Charlie and the Chocolate Factory

ROALD DAHL

Charlie and the Chocolate Factory

Illustrated by Quentin Blake

PUFFIN BOOKS

PUFFIN BOOKS
An imprint of Penguin Random House LLC
375 Hudson Street
New York, New York 10014

First published in the United States of America by Alfred A. Knopf, Inc., 1964
Published by Puffin Books by arrangement with Alfred A. Knopf, Inc., 1988
Reissued in this edition by Puffin Books,
an imprint of Penguin Random House LLC, 2016

THE LIBRARY OF CONGRESS HAS CATALOGED THE PREVIOUS PUFFIN BOOKS EDITION
UNDER CATALOG CARD NUMBER: 88-42886

Puffin Books ISBN 9780425287668

Printed in the United States of America

9 10 8

For Theo

CONTENTS

There are five children in this book:

AUGUSTUS GLOOP
A greedy boy

VERUCA SALT
A girl who is spoiled by her parents

VIOLET BEAUREGARDE
A girl who chews gum all day long

MIKE TEAVEE
A boy who does nothing but watch television

and

CHARLIE BUCKET
The hero

Charlie and the Chocolate Factory

1
Here Comes Charlie

THESE TWO VERY OLD PEOPLE are the father and mother of Mr. Bucket. Their names are Grandpa Joe and Grandma Josephine.

And *these* two very old people are the father and mother of Mrs. Bucket. Their names are Grandpa George and Grandma Georgina.

This is Mr. Bucket.   This is Mrs. Bucket.

Mr. and Mrs. Bucket have a small boy whose name is Charlie Bucket.

This is Charlie.

How d'you do? And how d'you do? And how d'you do again?

He is pleased to meet you.

The whole of this family—the six grownups (count them) and little Charlie Bucket—live together in a small wooden house on the edge of a great town.

The house wasn't nearly large enough for so many people, and life was extremely uncomfortable for them all. There were only two rooms in the place altogether, and there was only one bed. The bed was given to the four old grandparents because they were so old and tired. They were so tired, they never got out of it.

Grandpa Joe and Grandma Josephine on this side, Grandpa George and Grandma Georgina on this side.

Mr. and Mrs. Bucket and little Charlie Bucket slept in the other room, upon mattresses on the floor.

In the summertime, this wasn't too bad, but in the winter, freezing cold drafts blew across the floor all night long, and it was awful.

There wasn't any question of them being able to buy a better house—or even one more bed to sleep in. They were far too poor for that.

Mr. Bucket was the only person in the family with a job. He worked in a toothpaste factory, where he sat all day long at a bench and screwed the little caps onto the tops of the tubes of toothpaste after the tubes had been filled. But a toothpaste cap-screwer is never paid very much money, and poor Mr. Bucket, however hard he worked, and however fast he screwed on the caps, was never able to make enough to buy one-half of the things that so large a family needed. There wasn't even enough money to buy proper food for them all. The only meals they could afford were bread and margarine for breakfast, boiled potatoes and cabbage for lunch, and cabbage soup for supper. Sundays were a bit better. They all looked forward to Sundays because then, although they had exactly the same, everyone was allowed a second helping.

The Buckets, of course, didn't starve, but every one of them—the two old grandfathers, the two old grandmothers, Charlie's father, Charlie's mother, and especially little Charlie himself—went about from morning till night with a horrible empty feeling in their tummies.

Charlie felt it worst of all. And although his father and

mother often went without their own share of lunch or supper so that they could give it to him, it still wasn't nearly enough for a growing boy. He desperately wanted something more filling and satisfying than cabbage and cabbage soup. The one thing he longed for more than anything else was . . . CHOCOLATE.

Walking to school in the mornings, Charlie could see great slabs of chocolate piled up high in the shop windows, and he would stop and stare and press his nose against the glass, his mouth watering like mad. Many times a day, he would see other children taking creamy candy bars out of their pockets and munching them greedily, and *that*, of course, was *pure* torture.

Only once a year, on his birthday, did Charlie Bucket ever get to taste a bit of chocolate. The whole family saved up their money for that special occasion, and when the great day arrived, Charlie was always presented with one small chocolate bar to eat all by himself. And each time he received it, on those marvelous birthday mornings, he would place it carefully in a small wooden box that he owned, and treasure it as though it were a bar of solid gold; and for the next few days, he would allow himself only to look at it, but never to touch it. Then at last, when he could stand it no longer, he would peel back a *tiny* bit of the paper wrapping at one corner to expose a *tiny* bit of chocolate, and then he would take a *tiny* nibble—just enough to allow the lovely sweet taste to spread out slowly over his tongue. The next day, he would take another tiny nibble, and so on, and so on. And in this way, Charlie would make his ten-cent bar of birthday chocolate last him for more than a month.

But I haven't yet told you about the one awful thing that tortured little Charlie, the lover of chocolate, more than *anything* else. This thing, for him, was far, far worse than seeing slabs of chocolate in the shop windows or watching other children munching creamy candy bars right in front of him. It was the most terrible torturing thing you could imagine, and it was this:

In the town itself, actually within *sight* of the house in which Charlie lived, there was an ENORMOUS CHOCOLATE FACTORY!

Just imagine that!

And it wasn't simply an ordinary enormous chocolate factory, either. It was the largest and most famous in the whole world! It was WONKA'S FACTORY, owned by a man called Mr. Willy Wonka, the greatest inventor and maker of chocolates that there has ever been. And what a tremendous, marvelous place it was! It had huge iron gates leading in to it, and a high wall surrounding it, and smoke belching from its chimneys, and strange whizzing sounds coming from deep inside it. And outside the walls, for half a mile around in every direction, the air was scented with the heavy rich smell of melting chocolate!

Twice a day, on his way to and from school, little Charlie Bucket had to walk right past the gates of the factory. And every time he went by, he would begin to walk very, very slowly, and he would hold his nose high in the air and take long deep sniffs of the gorgeous chocolatey smell all around him.

Oh, how he loved that smell!

And oh, how he wished he could go inside the factory and see what it was like!

2
Mr. Willy Wonka's Factory

IN THE EVENINGS, after he had finished his supper of watery cabbage soup, Charlie always went into the room of his four grandparents to listen to their stories, and then afterwards to say good night.

Every one of these old people was over ninety. They were as shriveled as prunes, and as bony as skeletons, and throughout the day, until Charlie made his appearance, they lay huddled in their one bed, two at either end, with nightcaps on to keep their heads warm, dozing the time away with nothing to do. But as soon as they heard the door opening, and heard Charlie's voice saying, "Good evening, Grandpa Joe and Grandma Josephine, and Grandpa George and Grandma Georgina," then all four of them would suddenly sit up, and their old wrinkled faces would light up with smiles of pleasure—and the talking would begin. For they loved this little boy. He was the only bright thing in their lives, and his evening visits were something that they looked forward to all day long. Often, Charlie's mother and father would come in as well, and stand by the door, listening to the stories that the old people told; and thus, for perhaps half an hour every night, this room would become a happy place, and the whole family would forget that it was hungry and poor.

One evening, when Charlie went in to see his grandparents, he said to them, "Is it *really* true that Wonka's

Chocolate Factory is the biggest in the world?"

"*True?*" cried all four of them at once. "Of course it's true! Good heavens, didn't you know *that*? It's about *fifty* times as big as any other!"

"And is Mr. Willy Wonka *really* the cleverest chocolate maker in the world?"

"My *dear* boy," said Grandpa Joe, raising himself up a little higher on his pillow, "Mr. Willy Wonka is the most *amazing,* the most *fantastic,* the most *extraordinary* chocolate maker the world has ever seen! I thought *everybody* knew that!"

"I knew he was famous, Grandpa Joe, and I knew he was very clever. . . ."

"*Clever!*" cried the old man. "He's more than that! He's a *magician* with chocolate! He can make *anything*— anything he wants! Isn't that a fact, my dears?"

The other three old people nodded their heads slowly up and down, and said, "*Absolutely* true. *Just* as true as can be."

And Grandpa Joe said, "You mean to say I've never *told* you about Mr. Willy Wonka and his factory?"

"Never," answered little Charlie.

"Good heavens above! I don't know what's the matter with me!"

"Will you tell me now, Grandpa Joe, please?"

"I certainly will. Sit down beside me on the bed, my dear, and listen carefully."

Grandpa Joe was the oldest of the four grandparents. He was ninety-six and a half, and that is just about as old as anybody can be. Like all extremely old people, he was delicate and weak, and throughout the day he spoke very little. But in the evenings, when Charlie, his beloved grandson, was in the room, he seemed in some marvelous way to grow quite young again. All his tiredness fell away from him, and he became as eager and excited as a young boy.

"Oh, what a man he is, this Mr. Willy Wonka!" cried Grandpa Joe. "Did you know, for example, that he has himself invented more than two hundred new kinds of candy bars, each with a different center, each far sweeter and creamier and more delicious than anything the other chocolate factories can make!"

"Perfectly true!" cried Grandma Josephine. "And he sends them to *all* the four corners of the earth! Isn't that so, Grandpa Joe?"

"It is, my dear, it is. And to all the kings and presidents of the world as well. But it isn't only candy bars that he makes. Oh, dear me, no! He has some really *fantastic* inventions up his sleeve, Mr. Willy Wonka has! Did you know that he's invented a way of making chocolate ice cream so that it stays cold for hours and hours without being in the icebox?

You can even leave it lying in the sun all morning on a hot day and it won't go runny!"

"But that's *impossible*!" said little Charlie, staring at his grandfather.

"Of course it's impossible!" cried Grandpa Joe. "It's completely *absurd*! But Mr. Willy Wonka has done it!"

"Quite right!" the others agreed, nodding their heads. "Mr. Wonka has done it."

"And then again," Grandpa Joe went on, speaking very slowly now so that Charlie wouldn't miss a word, "Mr. Willy Wonka can make marshmallows that taste of violets, and rich caramels that change color every ten seconds as you suck them, and little feathery sweets that melt away deliciously the moment you put them between your lips. He can make chewing gum that never loses its taste, and candy balloons that you can blow up to enormous sizes before you pop them with a pin and gobble them up. And, by a most secret method, he can make lovely blue birds' eggs with black spots on them, and when you put one of these in your mouth, it gradually gets smaller

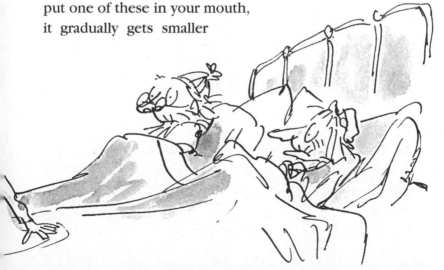

and smaller until suddenly there is nothing left except a tiny little pink sugary baby bird sitting on the tip of your tongue."

Grandpa Joe paused and ran the point of his tongue slowly over his lips. "It makes my mouth water just *thinking* about it," he said.

"Mine, too," said little Charlie. "But *please* go on."

While they were talking, Mr. and Mrs. Bucket, Charlie's mother and father, had come quietly into the room, and now both were standing just inside the door, listening.

"Tell Charlie about that crazy Indian prince," said Grandma Josephine. "He'd like to hear that."

"You mean Prince Pondicherry?" said Grandpa Joe, and he began chuckling with laughter.

"*Completely* dotty!" said Grandpa George.

"But *very* rich," said Grandma Georgina.

"What did he do?" asked Charlie eagerly.

"Listen," said Grandpa Joe, "and I'll tell you."

3

Mr. Wonka and the Indian Prince

"PRINCE PONDICHERRY wrote a letter to Mr. Willy Wonka," said Grandpa Joe, "and asked him to come all the way out to India and build him a colossal palace entirely out of chocolate."

"Did Mr. Wonka do it, Grandpa?"

"He did, indeed. And what a palace it was! It had one hundred rooms, and *everything* was made of either dark or light chocolate! The bricks were chocolate, and the cement holding them together was chocolate, and the windows were chocolate, and all the walls and ceilings were made of chocolate, so were the carpets and the pictures and the furniture and the beds; and when you turned on the taps in the bathroom, hot chocolate came pouring out.

"When it was all finished, Mr. Wonka said to Prince Pondicherry, 'I warn you, though, it won't last very long, so you'd better start eating it right away.'

"'Nonsense!' shouted the Prince. 'I'm not going to eat my palace! I'm not even going to nibble the staircase or lick the walls! I'm going to *live* in it!'

"But Mr. Wonka was right, of course, because soon after this, there came a very hot day with a boiling sun, and the whole palace began to melt, and then it sank slowly to the ground, and the crazy prince, who was dozing in the living room at the time, woke up to find himself swimming around in a huge brown sticky lake of chocolate."

Little Charlie sat very still on the edge of the bed, staring at his grandfather. Charlie's face was bright, and his eyes were stretched so wide you could see the whites all around. "Is all this *really* true?" he asked. "Or are you pulling my leg?"

"It's true!" cried all four of the old people at once. "Of course it's true! Ask anyone you like!"

"And I'll tell you something else that's true," said Grandpa Joe, and now he leaned closer to Charlie, and lowered his voice to a soft, secret whisper. *"Nobody . . . ever . . . comes . . . out!"*

"Out of where?" asked Charlie.

"And . . . nobody . . . ever . . . goes . . . in!"

"In *where*?" cried Charlie.

"Wonka's factory, of course!"

"Grandpa, what *do* you mean?"

"I mean *workers,* Charlie."

"Workers?"

"All factories," said Grandpa Joe, "have workers streaming in and out of the gates in the mornings and evenings —except Wonka's! Have *you* ever seen a single person going into that place—or coming out?"

Little Charlie looked slowly around at each of the four old faces, one after the other, and they all looked back at him. They were friendly smiling faces, but they were also quite serious. There was no sign of joking or leg-pulling on any of them.

"Well? Have *you*?" asked Grandpa Joe.

"I . . . I really don't know, Grandpa," Charlie stammered. "Whenever *I* walk past the factory, the gates seem to be closed."

"Exactly!" said Grandpa Joe.

"But there *must* be people working there. . . ."

"Not *people,* Charlie. Not *ordinary* people, anyway."

"Then who?" cried Charlie.

"Ah-ha. . . . That's it, you see. . . . That's another of Mr. Willy Wonka's clevernesses."

"Charlie, dear," Mrs. Bucket called out from where she was standing by the door, "it's time for bed. That's enough for tonight."

"But mother, I *must* hear. . . ."

"Tomorrow, my darling. . . ."

"That's right," said Grandpa Joe, "I'll tell you the rest of it tomorrow evening."

4
The Secret Workers

THE NEXT EVENING, Grandpa Joe went on with his story.

"You see, Charlie," he said, "not so very long ago there used to be thousands of people working in Mr. Willy Wonka's factory. Then one day, all of a sudden, Mr. Wonka had to ask *every single one of them* to leave, to go home, never to come back."

"But why?" asked Charlie.

"Because of spies."

"Spies?"

"Yes. All the other chocolate makers, you see, had begun to grow jealous of the wonderful candies that Mr. Wonka was making, and they started sending in spies to steal his secret recipes. The spies took jobs in the Wonka factory, pretending that they were ordinary workers, and while they were there, each one of them found out exactly how a certain special thing was made."

"And did they go back to their own factories and tell?" asked Charlie.

"They must have," answered Grandpa Joe, "because

soon after that, Fickelgruber's factory started making an ice cream that would never melt, even in the hottest sun. Then Mr. Prodnose's factory came out with a chewing gum that never lost its flavor however much you chewed it. And then Mr. Slugworth's factory began making candy balloons that you could blow up to huge sizes before you popped them with a pin and gobbled them up. And so on, and so on. And Mr. Willy Wonka tore his beard and shouted, 'This is terrible! I shall be ruined! There are spies everywhere! I shall have to close the factory!'"

"But he didn't do that!" Charlie said.

"Oh, yes he did. He told *all* the workers that he was sorry, but they would have to go home. Then, he shut the main gates and fastened them with a chain. And suddenly, Wonka's giant chocolate factory became silent and deserted. The chimneys stopped smoking, the machines stopped whirring, and from then on, not a single chocolate or candy was made. Not a soul went in or out, and even Mr. Willy Wonka himself disappeared completely.

"Months and months went by," Grandpa Joe went on, "but still the factory remained closed. And everybody said, 'Poor Mr. Wonka. He was so nice. And he made such marvelous things. But he's finished now. It's all over.'

"Then something astonishing happened. One day, early in the morning, thin columns of white smoke were seen to be coming out of the tops of the tall chimneys of the factory! People in the town stopped and stared. 'What's going on?' they cried. 'Someone's lit the furnaces! Mr. Wonka must be opening up again!' They ran to the gates, expecting to see them wide open and Mr. Wonka standing there to welcome his workers back.

"But no! The great iron gates were still locked and chained as securely as ever, and Mr. Wonka was nowhere to be seen.

"'But the factory *is* working!' the people shouted. 'Listen! You can hear the machines! They're all whirring again! And you can smell the smell of melting chocolate in the air!'"

Grandpa Joe leaned forward and laid a long bony finger on Charlie's knee, and he said softly, "But most mysterious of all, Charlie, were the shadows in the windows of the factory. The people standing on the street outside could see small dark shadows moving about behind the frosted glass windows."

"Shadows of whom?" said Charlie quickly.

"That's exactly what everybody else wanted to know.

"'The place is full of workers!' the people shouted. 'But nobody's gone in! The gates are locked! It's crazy! Nobody ever comes out, either!'"

"But there was no question at all," said Grandpa Joe, "that the factory *was* running. And it's gone on running ever since, for these last ten years. What's more, the chocolates and candies it's been turning out have become more fantastic and delicious all the time. And of course *now*, when Mr. Wonka invents some new and wonderful candy, neither Mr. Fickelgruber nor Mr. Prodnose nor Mr. Slugworth nor anybody else is able to copy it. No spies can go into the factory to find out how it is made."

"But Grandpa, *who*," cried Charlie, "*who* is Mr. Wonka using to do all the work in the factory?"

"Nobody knows, Charlie."

"But that's *absurd!* Hasn't someone asked Mr. Wonka?"

"Nobody sees him any more. He never comes out. The only things that come out of that place are chocolates and candies. They come out through a special trap door in the wall, all packed and addressed, and they are picked up every day by Post Office trucks."

"But Grandpa, what *sort* of people are they that work in there?"

"My dear boy," said Grandpa Joe, "that is one of the great mysteries of the chocolate-making world. We know only one thing about them. They are very small. The faint shadows that sometimes appear behind the windows, especially late at night when the lights are on, are those of *tiny* people, people no taller than my knee. . . ."

"There aren't any such people," Charlie said.

Just then, Mr. Bucket, Charlie's father, came into the room. He was home from the toothpaste factory, and he was waving an evening newspaper rather excitedly. "Have you heard the news?" he cried. He held up the paper so that they could see the huge headline. The headline said:

WONKA FACTORY TO BE OPENED AT LAST TO LUCKY FEW

5

The Golden Tickets

"YOU MEAN people are actually going to be allowed to go inside the factory?" cried Grandpa Joe. "Read us what it says—quickly!"

"All right," said Mr. Bucket, smoothing out the newspaper. "Listen."

Evening Bulletin

Mr. Willy Wonka, the candy-making genius whom nobody has seen for the last ten years, sent out the following notice today:

I, Willy Wonka, have decided to allow five children —just *five,* mind you, and no more—to visit my factory this year. These lucky five will be shown around personally by me, and they will be allowed to see all the secrets and the magic of my factory. Then, at the end of the tour, as a special present, all of them will be given enough chocolates and candies to last them for the rest of their lives! So watch out for the Golden Tickets! Five Golden Tickets have been printed on golden paper, and these five Golden Tickets have been hidden underneath the ordinary wrapping paper of five ordinary candy bars. These five candy bars may be anywhere—in any shop in any street in any town in any country in the world—upon any counter where Wonka's candies are sold. And the five lucky finders of these five Golden Tickets are the *only* ones who will be allowed to visit my factory and see what it's like *now* inside! Good luck to you all, and happy hunting! (Signed Willy Wonka.)

"The man's dotty!" muttered Grandma Josephine.

"He's brilliant!" cried Grandpa Joe. "He's a magician! Just imagine what will happen now! The whole world will be searching for those Golden Tickets! Everyone will be buying Wonka's candy bars in the hope of finding one! He'll sell more than ever before! Oh, how exciting it would be to find one!"

"And all the chocolate and candies that you could eat for the rest of your life—*free!*" said Grandpa George. "Just imagine that!"

"They'd have to deliver them in a truck!" said Grandma Georgina.

"It makes me quite ill to think of it," said Grandma Josephine.

"Nonsense!" cried Grandpa Joe. "Wouldn't it be *something,* Charlie, to open a bar of candy and see a Golden Ticket glistening inside!"

"It certainly would, Grandpa. But there isn't a hope," Charlie said sadly. "I only get one bar a year."

"You never know, darling," said Grandma Georgina. "It's your birthday next week. You have as much chance as anybody else."

"I'm afraid that simply isn't true," said Grandpa George. "The kids who are going to find the Golden Tickets are the ones who can afford to buy candy bars every day. Our Charlie gets only one a year. There isn't a hope."

6
The First Two Finders

THE VERY NEXT DAY, the first Golden Ticket was found. The finder was a boy called Augustus Gloop, and Mr. Bucket's evening newspaper carried a large picture of him on the front page. The picture showed a nine-year-old boy who was so enormously fat he looked as though he had been blown up with a powerful pump. Great flabby folds of fat bulged out from every part of his body, and his face was like a monstrous ball of dough with two small greedy curranty eyes peering out upon the world. The town in which Augustus Gloop lived, the newspaper said, had gone wild with excitement over their hero. Flags were flying from all the windows, children had been given a holiday from school, and a parade was being organized in honor of the famous youth.

"I just *knew* Augustus would find a Golden Ticket," his mother had told the newspapermen. "He eats *so many* candy bars a day that it was almost *impossible* for him *not* to find one. Eating is his hobby, you know. That's *all* he's interested in. But still, that's better than being a *hooligan* and shooting off *zip guns* and things like that in his spare time, isn't it? And what I always say is, he wouldn't go on eating like he does unless he *needed* nourishment, would he? It's all *vitamins,* anyway. What a *thrill* it will be for him to visit Mr. Wonka's marvelous factory! We're just as *proud* as can be!"

"What a revolting woman," said Grandma Josephine.

"And what a repulsive boy," said Grandma Georgina.

"Only four Golden Tickets left," said Grandpa George. "I wonder who'll get *those.*"

And now the whole country, indeed, the whole world, seemed suddenly to be caught up in a mad candy-buying spree, everybody searching frantically for those precious remaining tickets. Fully grown women were seen going into sweetshops and buying ten Wonka candy bars at a time, then tearing off the wrappers on the spot and peering eagerly underneath for a glint of golden paper. Children were taking hammers and smashing their piggy banks and running out to the shops with handfuls of money. In one city, a famous gangster robbed a bank of five thousand dollars and spent the whole lot on candy bars that same afternoon. And when the police entered his house to arrest him, they found him sitting on the floor amidst mountains of candy, ripping off the wrappers with the blade of a long dagger. In far-off Russia, a woman called Charlotte Russe claimed to have found the second ticket, but it turned out to be a clever fake. In England, the famous scientist, Professor Foulbody, invented a machine which would tell you at once, without opening the wrapper of a candy bar, whether or not there was a Golden Ticket hidden underneath it. The machine had a mechanical arm that shot out with tremendous force and grabbed hold of anything that had the slightest bit of gold inside it, and for a moment, it looked like the answer to everything. But unfortunately, while the Professor was showing off the machine to the public at the candy counter of a large department store, the mechanical arm shot out and made a grab for the gold filling in the back tooth of a duchess who was standing nearby. There was an ugly scene, and the machine was smashed by the crowd.

Suddenly, on the day before Charlie Bucket's birthday, the newspapers announced that the second Golden Ticket had been found. The lucky person was a small girl called Veruca Salt who lived with her rich parents in a great city far away. Once again, Mr. Bucket's evening newspaper carried a big picture of the finder. She was sitting between her beaming father and mother in the living room of their house, waving the Golden Ticket above her head, and grinning from ear to ear.

Veruca's father, Mr. Salt, had eagerly explained to the newspapermen exactly how the ticket was found. "You see, fellers," he had said, "as soon as my little girl told me that she simply *had* to have one of those Golden Tickets, I went out into the town and started buying up all the Wonka candy bars I could lay my hands on. *Thousands* of them, I must have bought. *Hundreds* of thousands! Then I had them loaded onto trucks and sent directly to my *own* factory. I'm in the peanut business, you see, and I've got about a hundred women working for me over at my joint, shelling peanuts for roasting and salting. That's what they do all day long, those women, they sit there shelling peanuts. So I says to them, 'Okay, girls,' I says, 'from now on, you can stop shelling peanuts and start shelling the wrappers off these crazy candy bars instead!' And they did. I had every worker in the place yanking the paper off those bars of chocolate full speed ahead from morning till night.

"But three days went by, and we had no luck. Oh, it was terrible! My little Veruca got more and more upset each day, and every time I went home she would scream at me, *'Where's my Golden Ticket! I want my Golden Ticket!'* And she would lie for hours on the floor, kicking and yelling in the most disturbing way. Well, sir, I just hated to see my little girl feeling unhappy like that, so I vowed I would keep up the search until I'd got her what she wanted. Then suddenly . . . on the evening of the fourth day, one of my women workers yelled, 'I've got it! A Golden Ticket!' And I said, 'Give it to me, quick!' and she did, and I rushed it home and gave it to my darling Veruca, and now she's all smiles, and we have a happy home once again."

"That's even worse than the fat boy," said Grandma Josephine.

"She needs a real good spanking," said Grandma Georgina.

"I don't think the girl's father played it quite fair, Grandpa, do you?" Charlie murmured.

"He spoils her," Grandpa Joe said. "And no good can ever come from spoiling a child like that, Charlie, you mark my words."

"Come to bed, my darling," said Charlie's mother. "Tomorrow's your birthday, don't forget that, so I expect you'll be up early to open your present."

"A Wonka candy bar!" cried Charlie. "It is a Wonka candy bar, isn't it?"

"Yes, my love," his mother said. "Of course it is."

"Oh, wouldn't it be wonderful if I found the third Golden Ticket inside it?" Charlie said.

"Bring it in here when you get it," Grandpa Joe said. "Then we can all watch you taking off the wrapper."

7

Charlie's Birthday

"HAPPY BIRTHDAY!" cried the four old grandparents as Charlie came into their room early the next morning.

Charlie smiled nervously and sat down on the edge of the bed. He was holding his present, his only present, very carefully in his two hands. WONKA'S WHIPPLE-SCRUMPTIOUS FUDGEMALLOW DELIGHT, it said on the wrapper.

The four old people, two at either end of the bed,

propped themselves up on their pillows and stared with anxious eyes at the candy bar in Charlie's hands.

Mr. and Mrs. Bucket came in and stood at the foot of the bed, watching Charlie.

The room became silent. Everybody was waiting now for Charlie to start opening his present. Charlie looked down at the candy bar. He ran his fingers slowly back and forth along the length of it, stroking it lovingly, and the shiny paper wrapper made little sharp crackly noises in the quiet room.

Then Mrs. Bucket said gently, "You mustn't be too disappointed, my darling, if you don't find what you're looking for underneath that wrapper. You really can't expect to be as lucky as all that."

"She's quite right," Mr. Bucket said.

Charlie didn't say anything.

"After all," Grandma Josephine said, "in the whole wide world there are only three tickets left to be found."

"The thing to remember," Grandma Georgina said, "is that whatever happens, you'll still have the bar of candy."

"Wonka's Whipple-Scrumptious Fudgemallow Delight!" cried Grandpa George. "It's the best of them all! You'll just *love* it!"

"Yes," Charlie whispered. "I know."

"Just forget all about those Golden Tickets and enjoy the candy," Grandpa Joe said. "Why don't you do that?"

They all knew it was ridiculous to expect this one poor little candy bar to have a magic ticket inside it, and they were trying as gently and as kindly as they could to prepare Charlie for the disappointment. But there was one other thing that the grownups also knew, and it was this: that however *small* the chance might be of striking lucky, *the chance was there.*

The chance *had* to be there.

This particular candy bar had as much chance as any other of having a Golden Ticket.

And that was why all the grandparents and parents in the room were actually just as tense and excited as Charlie was, although they were pretending to be very calm.

"You'd better go ahead and open it up, or you'll be late for school," Grandpa Joe said.

"You might as well get it over with," Grandpa George said.

"Open it, my dear," Grandma Georgina said. "Please open it. You're making me jumpy."

Very slowly, Charlie's fingers began to tear open one small corner of the wrapping paper.

The old people in the bed all leaned forward, craning their scraggy necks.

Then suddenly, as though he couldn't bear the suspense any longer, Charlie tore the wrapper right down the middle . . . and on to his lap, there fell . . . a light-brown creamy-colored chocolate candy bar.

There was no sign of a Golden Ticket anywhere.

"Well—that's *that!*" said Grandpa Joe brightly. "It's just what we expected."

Charlie looked up. Four kind old faces were watching him intently from the bed. He smiled at them, a small sad smile, and then he shrugged his shoulders and picked up the candy bar and held it out to his mother, and said, "Here Mother, have a bit. We'll share it. I want everybody to taste it."

"Certainly not!" his mother said.

And the others all cried, "No, no! We wouldn't dream of it! It's *all* yours!"

"*Please,*" begged Charlie, turning around and offering it to Grandpa Joe.

But neither he nor anyone else would take even a tiny bite.

"It's time to go to school, my darling," Mrs. Bucket said, putting an arm around Charlie's skinny shoulders. "Come on, or you'll be late."

8
Two More Golden Tickets Found

THAT EVENING, Mr. Bucket's newspaper announced the finding of not only the third Golden Ticket, but the fourth as well. TWO GOLDEN TICKETS FOUND TODAY, screamed the headlines. ONLY ONE MORE LEFT.

"All right," said Grandpa Joe, when the whole family was gathered in the old people's room after supper, "let's hear who found them."

"The third ticket," read Mr. Bucket, holding the newspaper up close to his face because his eyes were bad and he couldn't afford glasses, "the third Ticket was found by a Miss Violet Beauregarde. There was great excitement in the Beauregarde household when our reporter arrived to interview the lucky young lady—cameras were clicking and flashbulbs were flashing and people were pushing and jostling and trying to get a bit closer to the famous girl. And the famous girl was standing on a chair in the living-room waving the Golden Ticket madly at arm's length as though she were flagging a taxi. She was talking very fast and very loudly to everyone, but it was not easy to hear all that she said because she was chewing so ferociously upon a piece of gum at the same time.

"'I'm a gumchewer, normally,' she shouted, 'but when I heard about these ticket things of Mr. Wonka's, I laid off the gum and switched to candy bars in the hope of striking lucky. *Now,* of course, I'm right back on gum. I just *adore* gum. I can't do without it. I munch it all day long except for a few minutes at mealtimes when I take it out and stick it behind my ear for safekeeping. To tell you the honest truth, I simply wouldn't feel *comfortable* if I didn't have that little wedge of gum to chew on every moment of the day, I really wouldn't. My mother says it's not ladylike and it looks ugly to see a girl's jaws going up and down like mine do all the time, but I don't agree. And who's she to criticize, anyway, because if you ask me, I'd say that *her* jaws are going up and down almost as much as mine are just from *yelling* at me every minute of the day.'

"'Now, Violet,' Mrs. Beauregarde said from a far corner of the room where she was standing on the piano to avoid being trampled by the mob.

"'All right, Mother, keep your hair on!' Miss Beauregarde shouted. 'And now,' she went on, turning to the reporters again, 'it may interest you to know that this piece of gum I'm chewing right at this moment is one I've been working on for over *three months solid.* That's a record, that is. It's beaten the record held by my best friend, Miss Cornelia Prinzmetel. And was she mad! It's my most treasured possession now, this piece of gum is. At nights, I just stick it on the end of the bedpost, and it's as good as ever in the mornings—a bit hard at first, maybe, but it soon softens up again after I've given it a few good chews. Before I started chewing for the world record, I used to change my piece of gum once a day. I used to do it in our elevator on the way home from school. Why the elevator? Because I liked sticking the gooey piece that I'd just finished with onto one of the elevator buttons. Then the next person who came along and pressed the button got my old gum on the end of his or her finger. Ha-ha! And what a racket they kicked up, some of them. You get the best results with women who have expensive gloves on. Oh yes, I'm thrilled to be going to Mr. Wonka's factory. And I understand that afterwards he's going to give me enough gum to last me for the rest of my whole life. Whoopee! Hooray!"

"*Beastly* girl," said Grandma Josephine.

"Despicable!" said Grandma Georgina. "She'll come to a sticky end one day, chewing all that gum, you see if she doesn't."

"And who got the fourth Golden Ticket, Daddy?" Charlie asked.

"Now, let me see," said Mr. Bucket, peering at the newspaper again. "Ah yes, here we are. The fourth Golden Ticket," he read, "was found by a boy called Mike Teavee."

"Another bad lot, I'll be bound," muttered Grandma Josephine.

"Don't interrupt, Grandma," said Mrs. Bucket.

"The Teavee household," said Mr. Bucket, going on with his reading, "was crammed, like all the others, with excited visitors when our reporter arrived, but young Mike Teavee, the lucky winner, seemed extremely annoyed by the whole business. 'Can't you fools see I'm watching television?' he said angrily, 'I wish you wouldn't interrupt!'

"The nine-year-old boy was seated before an enormous television set, with his eyes glued to the screen, and he was watching a film in which one bunch of gangsters was shooting up another bunch of gangsters with machine guns. Mike Teavee himself had no less than eighteen toy pistols of various sizes hanging from belts around his body, and every now and again he would leap up into the air and fire off half a dozen rounds from one or another of these weapons.

"'Quiet!' he shouted, when someone tried to ask him a question. 'Didn't I *tell* you not to interrupt! This show's an absolute whiz-banger! It's terrific! I watch it every day. I watch all of them every day, even the crummy ones, where there's no shooting. I like the gangsters best.

They're terrific, those gangsters! Especially when they start pumping each other full of lead, or flashing the old stilettos, or giving each other the one-two-three with their knuckle-dusters! Oh boy, what wouldn't I give to be doing that myself! It's the *life*, I tell you! It's terrific!'"

"That's quite enough!" snapped Grandma Josephine. "I can't *bear* to listen to it!"

"Nor me," said Grandma Georgina. "Do *all* children behave like this nowadays—like these brats we've been hearing about?"

"Of course not," said Mr. Bucket, smiling at the old lady in the bed. "Some do, of course. In fact, quite a lot of them do. But not *all.*"

"And now there's only *one ticket left!*" said Grandpa George.

"Quite so," sniffed Grandma Georgina. "And just as sure as I'll be having cabbage soup for supper tomorrow, that ticket'll go to some nasty little beast who doesn't deserve it!"

9
Grandpa Joe Takes a Gamble

THE NEXT DAY, when Charlie came home from school and went in to see his grandparents, he found that only Grandpa Joe was awake. The other three were all snoring loudly.

"Ssshh!" whispered Grandpa Joe, and he beckoned Charlie to come closer. Charlie tiptoed over and stood beside the bed. The old man gave Charlie a sly grin, and then he started rummaging under his pillow with one hand; and when the hand came out again, there was an ancient leather purse clutched in the fingers. Under cover of the bedclothes, the old man opened the purse and tipped it upside down. Out fell a single silver ten-cent piece. "It's my secret hoard," he whispered. "The others don't know I've got it. And now, you and I are going to have one more fling at finding that last ticket. How about it, eh? But you'll have to help me."

"Are you *sure* you want to spend your money on that, Grandpa?" Charlie whispered.

"Of course I'm sure!" spluttered the old man excitedly. "Don't stand there arguing! I'm just as crazy as you are to find that ticket! Here—take the money and run down the street to the nearest store and buy the first Wonka candy bar you see and bring it straight back to me, and we'll open it together."

Charlie took the little silver coin, and slipped quickly out of the room. In five minutes, he was back.

"Have you got it?" whispered Grandpa Joe, his eyes shining with excitement.

Charlie nodded and held out the bar of candy. WONKA'S NUTTY CRUNCH SURPRISE, it said on the wrapper.

"Good!" the old man whispered, sitting up in the bed and rubbing his hands. "Now—come over here and sit close to me and we'll open it together. Are you ready?"

"Yes," Charlie said. "I'm ready."

"All right. You tear off the first bit."

"No," Charlie said, "you paid for it. You do it all."

The old man's fingers were trembling most terribly as they fumbled with the candy bar. "We don't have a hope, really," he whispered, giggling a bit. "You do know we don't have a hope, don't you?"

"Yes," Charlie said. "I know that."

They looked at each other, and both started giggling nervously.

"Mind you," said Grandpa Joe, "there is just that *tiny* chance that it *might* be the one, don't you agree?"

"Yes," Charlie said. "Of course. Why don't you open it Grandpa?"

"All in good time, my boy, all in good time. Which end do you think I ought to open first?"

"That corner. The one furthest from you. Just tear off a *tiny* bit, but not quite enough for us to see anything."

"Like that?" said the old man.

"Yes. Now a little bit more."

"You finish it," said Grandpa Joe. "I'm too nervous."

"No, Grandpa. You must do it yourself."

"Very well, then. Here goes." He tore off the wrapper.

They both stared at what lay underneath.

It was a bar of candy—nothing more.

All at once, they both saw the funny side of the whole thing, and they burst into peals of laughter.

"What the heck's going on!" cried Grandma Josephine, waking up suddenly.

"Nothing," said Grandpa Joe. "You go on back to sleep."

10
The Family Begins to Starve

DURING THE NEXT TWO WEEKS, the weather turned very cold. First came the snow. It began very suddenly one morning just as Charlie Bucket was getting dressed for school. Standing by the window, he saw the huge flakes drifting slowly down out of an icy sky that was the color of steel.

By evening, it lay four feet deep around the tiny house, and Mr. Bucket had to dig a path from the front door to the road.

After the snow, there came a freezing gale that blew for days and days without stopping. And oh, how bitter cold it was! Everything that Charlie touched seemed to be made of ice, and each time he stepped outside the door, the wind was like a knife on his cheek.

Inside the house, little jets of freezing air came rushing in through the sides of the windows and under the doors, and there was no place to go to escape them. The four old ones lay silent and huddled in their bed, trying to keep the cold out of their bones. The excitement over the Golden Tickets had long since been forgotten. Nobody in the family gave a thought now to anything except the two vital problems of trying to keep warm and trying to get enough to eat.

There is something about very cold weather that gives one an enormous appetite. Most of us find ourselves beginning to crave rich steaming stews and hot apple pies and all kinds of delicious warming dishes; and because we are all a great deal luckier than we realize, we usually get what we want—or near enough. But Charlie Bucket never got what he wanted because the family couldn't afford it, and as the cold weather went on and on, he became ravenously and desperately hungry. Both bars of candy, the birthday one and the one Grandpa Joe had bought, had long since been nibbled away, and all he got now were those thin, cabbagy meals three times a day.

Then all at once, the meals became even thinner.

The reason for this was that the toothpaste factory, the place where Mr. Bucket worked, suddenly went bust and had to close down. Quickly, Mr. Bucket tried to get another job. But he had no luck. In the end, the only way in which he managed to earn a few pennies was by shoveling snow in the streets. But it wasn't enough to buy even a quarter of the food that seven people needed. The situation became desperate. Breakfast was a single slice of bread for each person now, and lunch was maybe half a boiled potato.

Slowly but surely, everybody in the house began to starve.

And every day, little Charlie Bucket, trudging through the snow on his way to school, would have to pass Mr. Willy Wonka's giant chocolate factory. And every day, as he came near to it, he would lift his small pointed nose high in the air and sniff the wonderful sweet smell of melting chocolate. Sometimes, he would stand motionless outside the gates for several minutes on end, taking deep swallowing breaths as though he were trying to *eat* the smell itself.

"That child," said Grandpa Joe, poking his head up from under the blanket one icy morning, "that child has

got to have more food. It doesn't matter about us. We're too old to bother with. But a *growing boy!* He can't go on like this! He's beginning to look like a skeleton!"

"What can one *do?*" murmured Grandma Josephine miserably. "He refuses to take any of ours. I hear his mother tried to slip her own piece of bread onto his plate at breakfast this morning, but he wouldn't touch it. He made her take it back."

"He's a fine little fellow," said Grandpa George. "He deserves better than this."

The cruel weather went on and on.

And every day, Charlie Bucket grew thinner and thinner. His face became frighteningly white and pinched. The skin was drawn so tightly over the cheeks that you could see the shapes of the bones underneath. It seemed doubtful whether he could go on much longer like this without becoming dangerously ill.

And now, very calmly, with that curious wisdom that seems to come so often to small children in times of hardship, he began to make little changes here and there in some of the things that he did, so as to save his strength. In the mornings, he left the house ten minutes earlier so that he could walk slowly to school, without ever having to run. He sat quietly in the classroom during recess, resting himself, while the others rushed outdoors and threw snowballs and wrestled in the snow. Everything he did now, he did slowly and carefully, to prevent exhaustion.

Then one afternoon, walking back home with the icy wind in his face (and incidentally feeling hungrier than he had ever felt before), his eye was caught suddenly by a piece of paper that was lying in the gutter, in the snow.

The paper was of a greenish color, and there was something vaguely familiar about it. Charlie stepped off the curb and bent down to examine it. Part of it was buried under the snow, but he saw at once what it was.

It was a dollar bill!

Quickly he looked around him.

Had somebody just dropped it?

No—that was impossible because of the way part of it was buried.

Several people went hurrying past him on the sidewalk, their chins sunk deep in the collars of their coats, their feet crunching in the snow. None of them was searching for any money; none of them was taking the slightest notice of the small boy crouching in the gutter.

Then was it *his,* this dollar?

Could he *have* it?

Carefully, Charlie pulled it out from under the snow. It was damp and dirty, but otherwise perfect.

A WHOLE dollar!

He held it tightly between his shivering fingers, gazing down at it. It meant one thing to him at that moment, only *one* thing. It meant FOOD.

Automatically, Charlie turned and began moving toward the nearest shop. It was only ten paces away . . . it was a newspaper and stationery store, the kind that sells almost everything, including candy and cigars . . . and what he would *do,* he whispered quickly to himself . . . he would buy one luscious bar of candy and eat it *all* up, every bit of it, right then and there . . . and the rest of the money he would take straight back home and give to his mother.

11

The Miracle

CHARLIE ENTERED THE STORE and laid the damp dollar bill on the counter.

"One Wonka's Whipple-Scrumptious Fudgemallow Delight," he said, remembering how much he had loved the one he had on his birthday.

The man behind the counter looked fat and well-fed. He had big lips and fat cheeks and a very fat neck. The fat around his neck bulged out all around the top of his collar like a rubber ring. He turned and reached behind him

for the candy bar, then he turned back again and handed it to Charlie. Charlie grabbed it and quickly tore off the wrapper and took an enormous bite. Then he took another . . . and another . . . and oh, the joy of being able to cram large pieces of something sweet and solid into one's mouth! The sheer blissful joy of being able to fill one's mouth with rich solid food!

"You look like you wanted that one, sonny," the shopkeeper said pleasantly.

Charlie nodded, his mouth bulging with chocolate

The shopkeeper put Charlie's change on the counter. "Take it easy," he said. "It'll give you a gut-ache if you swallow it like that without chewing."

Charlie went on wolfing the candy. He couldn't stop.

And in less than half a minute, the whole thing had disappeared down his throat. He was quite out of breath, but he felt marvelously, extraordinarily happy. He reached out a hand to take the change. Then he paused. His eyes were just above the level of the counter. They were staring at the little silver coins lying there. The coins were all dimes. There were nine of them altogether. Surely it wouldn't matter if he spent just one more. . . .

"I think," he said quietly, "I think . . . I'll have just one more of those candy bars. The same kind as before, please."

"Why not?" the fat shopkeeper said, reaching behind him again and taking another Whipple-Scrumptious Fudgemallow Delight from the shelf. He laid it on the counter.

Charlie picked it up and tore off the wrapper . . . and *suddenly* . . . from underneath the wrapper . . . there came a brilliant flash of gold.

Charlie's heart stood still.

"It's a Golden Ticket!" screamed the shopkeeper, leaping about a foot in the air. "You've got a Golden Ticket! You've found the last Golden Ticket! Hey, what do you know! Come and look at this, everybody! The kid's found Wonka's last Golden Ticket! There it is! It's right there in his hands!"

It seemed as though the shopkeeper might be going to have a fit. "In my shop, too!" he yelled. "He found it right here in my own little shop! Somebody call the newspapers quick and let them know! Watch out now, sonny! Don't tear it as you unwrap it! That thing's precious!"

In a few seconds, there was a crowd of about twenty people clustering around Charlie, and many more were pushing their way in from the street. Everybody wanted to get a look at the Golden Ticket and at the lucky finder.

"Where is it?" somebody shouted. "Hold it up so all of us can see it!"

"There it is, there!" someone else shouted. "He's holding it in his hands! See the gold shining!"

"How did *he* manage to find it, I'd like to know?" a large boy shouted angrily. "*Twenty* bars a day I've been buying for weeks and weeks!"

"Think of all the free stuff he'll be getting too!" another boy said enviously. "A lifetime supply!"

"He'll need it, the skinny little shrimp!" a girl said, laughing.

Charlie hadn't moved. He hadn't even unwrapped the Golden Ticket from around the candy bar. He was standing very still, holding it tightly with both hands while the crowd pushed and shouted all around him. He felt quite dizzy. There was a peculiar floating sensation coming over him, as though he were floating up in the air like a balloon. His feet didn't seem to be touching the ground at all. He could hear his heart thumping away loudly somewhere in his throat.

At that point, he became aware of a hand resting lightly on his shoulder, and when he looked up, he saw a tall man standing over him. "Listen," the man whispered. "I'll buy it from you. I'll give you fifty dollars. How about it, eh? And I'll give you a new bicycle as well. Okay?"

"Are you *crazy*?" shouted a woman who was standing equally close. "Why, I'd give him *five hundred* dollars for that ticket! You want to sell that ticket for five hundred dollars, young man?"

"That's *quite* enough of that!" the fat shopkeeper

shouted, pushing his way through the crowd and taking Charlie firmly by the arm. "Leave the kid alone, will you! Make way there! Let him out!" And to Charlie, as he led him to the door, he whispered, "Don't you let *anybody* have it! Take it straight home, quickly, before you lose it! Run all the way and don't stop till you get there, you understand?"

Charlie nodded.

"You know something," the fat shopkeeper said, pausing a moment and smiling at Charlie, "I have a feeling you needed a break like this. I'm awfully glad you got it. Good luck to you, sonny."

"Thank you," Charlie said, and off he went, running through the snow as fast as his legs would go. And as he flew past Mr. Willy Wonka's factory, he turned and waved at it and sang out, "I'll be seeing you! I'll be seeing you soon!" And five minutes later he arrived at his own home.

12
What It Said on the Golden Ticket

CHARLIE BURST THROUGH the front door, shouting, *"Mother! Mother! Mother!"*

Mrs. Bucket was in the old grandparents' room, serving them their evening soup.

"Mother!" yelled Charlie, rushing in on them like a hur-

ricane. "Look! I've got it! Look, Mother, look! The last Golden Ticket! It's mine! I found some money in the street and I bought two candy bars and the second one had the Golden Ticket and there were *crowds* of people all around me wanting to see it and the shopkeeper rescued me and I ran all the way home and here I am! *IT'S THE FIFTH GOLDEN TICKET, MOTHER, AND I'VE FOUND IT!*"

Mrs. Bucket simply stood and stared, while the four old grandparents, who were sitting up in bed balancing bowls of soup on their laps, all dropped their spoons with a clatter and froze against their pillows.

For about ten seconds there was absolute silence in the room. Nobody dared to speak or move. It was a magic moment.

Then, very softly, Grandpa Joe said, "You're pulling our legs, Charlie, aren't you? You're having a little joke?"

"I am *not*!" cried Charlie, rushing up to the bed and holding out the large and beautiful Golden Ticket for him to see.

Grandpa Joe leaned forward and took a close look, his nose almost touching the ticket. The others watched him, waiting for the verdict.

Then very slowly, with a slow and marvelous grin spreading all over his face, Grandpa Joe lifted his head and looked straight at Charlie. The color was rushing to his cheeks, and his eyes were wide open, shining with joy, and in the center of each eye, right in the very center, in the black pupil, a little spark of wild excitement was slowly dancing. Then the old man took a deep breath, and suddenly, with no warning whatsoever, an explosion seemed to take place inside him. He threw up his arms

and yelled *"Yippeeeeeeeeeeeeeeeeeeeeeeeeee!"* And at the same time, his long bony body rose up out of the bed and his bowl of soup went flying into the face of Grandma Josephine, and in one fantastic leap, this old fellow of ninety-six and a half, who hadn't been out of bed these last twenty years, jumped on to the floor and started doing a dance of victory in his pajamas.

"Yippeeeeeeeeee!" he shouted. "Three cheers for Charlie! Hip, hip, hooray!"

At this point, the door opened, and Mr. Bucket walked into the room. He was cold and tired, and he looked it. All day long, he had been shoveling snow in the streets.

"Cripes!" he cried. "What's going on in here?"

It didn't take them long to tell him what had happened.

"I don't believe it!" he said. "It's not possible."

"Show him the ticket, Charlie!" shouted Grandpa Joe, who was still dancing around the floor like a dervish in his striped pajamas. "Show your father the fifth and last Golden Ticket in the world!"

"Let me see it, Charlie," Mr. Bucket said, collapsing into a chair and holding out his hand. Charlie came forward with the precious document.

It was a very beautiful thing, this Golden Ticket, having been made, so it seemed, from a sheet of pure gold hammered out almost to the thinness of paper. On one side of it, printed by some clever method in jet-black letters, was the invitation itself—from Mr. Wonka.

"Read it aloud," said Grandpa Joe, climbing back into bed again at last. "Let's all hear exactly what it says."

Mr. Bucket held the lovely Golden Ticket up close

to his eyes. His hands were trembling slightly, and he seemed to be overcome by the whole business. He took several deep breaths. Then he cleared his throat, and said, "All right, I'll read it. Here we go:

'Greetings to you, the lucky finder of this golden ticket, from Mr. Willy Wonka! I shake you warmly by the hand! Tremendous things are in store for you! Many wonderful surprises await you! For now, I do invite you to come to my factory and be my guest for one whole day—you and all others who are lucky enough to find my Golden Tickets. I, Willy Wonka, will conduct you around the factory myself, showing you everything that there is to see, and afterwards, when it is time to leave, you will be escorted home by a procession of large trucks. These trucks, I can promise you, will be loaded with enough delicious eatables to last you and your entire household for many years. If, at any time thereafter, you should run out of supplies, you have only to come back to the factory and show this Golden Ticket, and I shall be happy to refill your cupboard with whatever you want. In this way, you will be able to keep yourself supplied with tasty morsels for the rest of your life. But this is by no means the most exciting thing that will happen on the day of your visit. I am preparing other surprises that are even more marvelous and more fantastic for you and for all my beloved Golden Ticket holders—mystic and marvelous surprises that will entrance, delight, intrigue, astonish, and perplex you beyond measure. In your wildest

dreams you could not imagine that such things could happen to you! Just wait and see! And now, here are your instructions: The day I have chosen for the visit is the first day in the month of February. On this day, and on no other, you must come to the factory gates at ten o'clock sharp in the morning. Don't be late! And you are allowed to bring with you either one or two members of your own family to look after you and to ensure that you don't get into mischief. One more thing—be certain to have this ticket with you, otherwise you will not be admitted.

(Signed) Willy Wonka.'"

"The first day of *February*!" cried Mrs. Bucket. "But that's *tomorrow*! Today is the last day of January, *I know it is!*"

"Cripes!" said Mr. Bucket. "I think you're right!"

"You're just in time!" shouted Grandpa Joe. "There's not a moment to lose. You must start making preparations at once! Wash your face, comb your hair, scrub your hands, brush your teeth, blow your nose, cut your nails, polish your shoes, iron your shirt, and for heaven's sake, get all that mud off your pants! You must get ready, my boy! You must get ready for the biggest day of your life!"

"Now don't overexcite yourself, Grandpa," Mrs. Bucket said. "And don't fluster poor Charlie. We must all try to keep very calm. Now the first thing to decide is this— who is going to go with Charlie to the factory?"

"*I* will!" shouted Grandpa Joe, leaping out of bed once again. "I'll take him! I'll look after him! You leave it to me!"

Mrs. Bucket smiled at the old man, then she turned to her husband and said, "How about you, dear? Don't you think *you* ought to go?"

"Well . . ." Mr. Bucket said, pausing to think about it, "no . . . I'm not so sure that I should."

"But you *must*."

"There's no *must* about it, my dear," Mr. Bucket said gently. "Mind you, I'd *love* to go. It'll be tremendously exciting. But on the other hand . . . I believe that the person who really *deserves* to go most of all is Grandpa Joe himself. He seems to know more about it than we do. Provided, of course, that he feels well enough. . . ."

"Yippeeeeee!" shouted Grandpa Joe, seizing Charlie by the hands and dancing round the room.

"He certainly *seems* well enough," Mrs. Bucket said, laughing. "Yes . . . perhaps you're right after all. Perhaps

Grandpa Joe should be the one to go with him. I certainly can't go myself and leave the other three old people all alone in bed for a whole day."

"Hallelujah!" yelled Grandpa Joe. "Praise the Lord!"

At that point, there came a loud knock on the front door. Mr. Bucket went to open it, and the next moment, swarms of newspapermen and photographers were pouring into the house. They had tracked down the finder of the fifth Golden Ticket, and now they all wanted to get the full story for the front pages of morning papers. For several hours, there was complete pandemonium in the little house, and it must have been nearly midnight before Mr. Bucket was able to get rid of them so that Charlie could go to bed.

13
The Big Day Arrives

THE SUN WAS SHINING BRIGHTLY on the morning of the big day, but the ground was still white with snow and the air was very cold.

Outside the gates of Wonka's factory, enormous crowds of people had gathered to watch the five lucky ticket holders going in. The excitement was tremendous. It was just before ten o'clock. The crowds were pushing and shouting, and policemen with arms linked were trying to hold them back from the gates.

Right beside the gates, in a small group that was carefully shielded from the crowds by the police, stood the five famous children, together with the grownups who had come with them.

The tall bony old figure of Grandpa Joe could be seen standing quietly among them, and beside him, holding tightly on to his hand, was little Charlie Bucket himself.

All the children, except Charlie, had both their mothers and fathers with them, and it was a good thing that they had, otherwise the whole party might have gotten out of hand. They were so eager to get going that their parents were having to hold them back by force to prevent them from climbing over the gates. "Be patient!" cried the fathers. "Be still! It's not *time* yet! It's not ten o'clock!"

Behind him, Charlie Bucket could hear the shouts of the people in the crowd as they pushed and fought to get a glimpse of the famous children.

"There's Violet Beauregarde!" he heard someone shouting. "That's her all right! I can remember her face from the newspapers!"

"And you know what?" somebody else shouted back. "She's still chewing that dreadful old piece of gum she's had for three months! You look at her jaws! They're still working on it!"

"Who's the big fat boy?"

"That's Augustus Gloop!"

"So it is!"

"Enormous, isn't he!"

"Fantastic!"

"Who's the kid with a picture of The Lone Ranger stenciled on his windbreaker?"

"That's Mike Teavee! He's the television fiend!"

"He must be crazy! Look at all those crazy pistols he's got hanging all over him!"

"The one *I* want to see is Veruca Salt!" shouted another voice in the crowd. "She's the girl whose father bought up half a million candy bars and then made the workers in his peanut factory unwrap every one of them until they found a Golden Ticket! He gives her anything she wants! Absolutely anything! She only has to start scream-ing for it and she gets it!"

"Dreadful, isn't it?"

"Shocking, I call it!"

"Which do you think is her?"

"That one! Over there on the left! The little girl in the silver mink coat!"

"Which one is Charlie Bucket?"

"Charlie Bucket? He must be that skinny little shrimp standing beside the old fellow who looks like a skeleton. Right close to us. Just there! See him?"

"Why hasn't he got a coat on in this cold weather?"

"Don't ask me. Maybe he can't afford to buy one."

"Jeepers! He must be freezing!"

Charlie, standing only a few paces away from the speaker, gave Grandpa Joe's hand a squeeze, and the old man looked down at Charlie and smiled.

Somewhere in the distance, a church clock began striking ten.

Very slowly, with a loud creaking of rusty hinges, the

great iron gates of the factory began to swing open.

The crowd became suddenly silent. The children stopped jumping about. All eyes were fixed upon the gates.

"There he is!" somebody shouted. *"That's him!"*

And so it was!

14
Mr. Willy Wonka

MR. WONKA WAS STANDING all alone just inside the open gates of the factory.

And what an extraordinary little man he was!

He had a black top hat on his head.

He wore a tail coat made of a beautiful plum-colored velvet.

His trousers were bottle green.

His gloves were pearly gray.

And in one hand he carried a fine gold-topped walking cane.

Covering his chin, there was a small neat pointed black beard—a goatee. And his eyes—his eyes were most marvelously bright. They seemed to be sparkling and twinkling at you all the time. The whole face, in fact, was alight with fun and laughter.

And oh, how clever he looked! How quick and sharp and full of life! He kept making quick jerky little movements with his head, cocking it this way and that, and taking everything in with those bright twinkling eyes. He was like a squirrel in the quickness of his movements, like a quick clever old squirrel from the park.

Suddenly, he did a funny little skipping dance in the snow, and he spread his arms wide, and he smiled at the five children who were clustered near the gates, and he called out, "Welcome, my little friends! Welcome to the factory!"

His voice was high and flutey. "Will you come forward one at a time, please," he called out, "and bring your parents. Then show me your Golden Ticket and give me your name. Who's first?"

The big fat boy stepped up. "I'm Augustus Gloop," he said.

"Augustus!" cried Mr. Wonka, seizing his hand and pumping it up and down with terrific force. "My *dear* boy, how *good* to see you! Delighted! Charmed! Overjoyed to have you with us! And *these* are your parents? How nice! Come in! Come in! That's right! Step through the gates!"

Mr. Wonka was clearly just as excited as everybody else.

"My name," said the next child to go forward, "is Veruca Salt."

"My *dear* Veruca! How *do* you do? What a pleasure this is! You *do* have an interesting name, don't you? I always thought that a veruca was a sort of wart that you got on the sole of your foot! But I must be wrong, mustn't I? How pretty you look in that lovely mink coat! I'm so glad you could come! Dear me, this is going to be *such* an exciting day! I *do* hope you enjoy it! I'm sure you *will*! I *know* you will! Your father? How *are* you, Mr. Salt? And Mrs. Salt? Overjoyed to see you! Yes, the ticket is *quite* in order! Please go in!"

The next two children, Violet Beauregarde and Mike Teavee, came forward to have their tickets examined and then to have their arms practically pumped off their shoulders by the energetic Mr. Wonka.

And last of all, a small nervous voice whispered, "Charlie Bucket."

"Charlie!" cried Mr. Wonka. "Well, well, well! So *there*

you are! You're the one who found your ticket only yesterday, aren't you? Yes, yes. I read *all* about it in this morning's papers! *Just* in time, my dear boy! I'm so glad! So happy for you! And this? Your grandfather? Delighted to meet you, sir! Overjoyed! Enraptured! Enchanted! All right! Excellent! Is everybody in now? Five children? Yes! Good! Now will you please follow me! Our tour is about to begin! But *do* keep together! *Please* don't wander off by yourselves! I shouldn't like to lose any of you at *this* stage of the proceedings! Oh, dear me, no!"

Charlie glanced back over his shoulder and saw the great iron entrance gates slowly closing behind him. The crowds on the outside were still pushing and shouting. Charlie took a last look at them. Then, as the gates closed with a clang, all sight of the outside world disappeared.

"Here we are!" cried Mr. Wonka, trotting along in front of the group. "Through this big red door, please! *That's* right! It's nice and warm inside! I have to keep it warm inside the factory because of the workers! My workers are used to an *extremely* hot climate! They can't stand the cold! They'd perish if they went outdoors in this weather! They'd freeze to death!"

"But who *are* these workers?" asked Augustus Gloop.

"All in good time, my dear boy!" said Mr. Wonka, smiling at Augustus. "Be patient! You shall see everything as we go along! Are all of you inside? Good! Would you mind closing the door? Thank you."

Charlie Bucket found himself standing in a long corridor that stretched away in front of him as far as he could see. The corridor was so wide that a car could easily have been driven along it. The walls were pale pink, the lighting was soft and pleasant.

"How lovely and warm!" whispered Charlie.

"I know. And what a marvelous smell!" answered Grandpa Joe, taking a long deep sniff. All the most wonderful smells in the world seemed to be mixed up in the air around them—the smell of roasting coffee and burnt sugar and melting chocolate and mint and violets and crushed hazelnuts and apple blossom and caramel and lemon peel. . . .

And far away in the distance, from the heart of the great factory, came a muffled roar of energy as though some monstrous gigantic machine were spinning its wheels at breakneck speed.

"Now *this,* my dear children," said Mr. Wonka, raising his voice above the noise, "this is the main corridor. Will you please hang your coats and hats on those pegs over there, and then follow me. *That's* the way! Good! Everyone ready! Come on, then! Here we go!" He trotted off rapidly down the corridor with the tails of his plum-colored velvet coat flapping behind him, and the visitors all hurried after him.

It was quite a large party of people, when you came to think of it. There were nine grownups and five children, fourteen in all. So you can imagine that there was a good deal of pushing and shoving as they hustled and bustled down the passage, trying to keep up with the swift little figure in front of them. "Come *on!*" cried Mr. Wonka. "Get a move on, please! We'll *never* get round today if you dawdle like this!"

Soon, he turned right off the main corridor into another slightly narrower passage.

Then he turned left.

Then left again.

Then right.

Then left.

Then right.

Then right.

Then left.

The place was like a gigantic rabbit warren, with passages leading this way and that in every direction.

"Don't you let go my hand, Charlie," whispered Grandpa Joe.

"Notice how all these passages are sloping downwards!" called Mr. Wonka. "We are now going underground! *All* the most important rooms in my factory are deep down below the surface!"

"Why is that?" somebody asked.

"There wouldn't be *nearly* enough space for them up on top!" answered Mr. Wonka. "These rooms we are going to see are *enormous*! They're larger than football fields! No building in the *world* would be big enough to house them! But down here, underneath the ground, I've got *all* the space I want. There's no limit—so long as I hollow it out."

Mr. Wonka turned right.

He turned left.

He turned right again.

The passages were sloping steeper and steeper downhill now.

Then suddenly, Mr. Wonka stopped. In front of him, there was a shiny metal door. The party crowded round. On the door, in large letters, it said:

THE CHOCOLATE ROOM

15

The Chocolate Room

"AN IMPORTANT ROOM, THIS!" cried Mr. Wonka, taking a bunch of keys from his pocket and slipping one into the keyhole of the door. "*This* is the nerve center of the whole factory, the heart of the whole business! And so *beautiful*! I *insist* upon my rooms being beautiful! I can't *abide* ugliness in factories! *In* we go, then! But *do* be careful, my dear children! Don't lose your heads! Don't get overexcited! Keep very calm!"

Mr. Wonka opened the door. Five children and nine grownups pushed their ways in—and *oh,* what an amazing sight it was that now met their eyes!

They were looking down upon a lovely valley. There were green meadows on either side of the valley, and along the bottom of it there flowed a great brown river.

What is more, there was a tremendous waterfall halfway along the river—a steep cliff over which the water curled and rolled in a solid sheet, and then went crashing down into a boiling churning whirlpool of froth and spray.

Below the waterfall (and this was the most astonishing sight of all), a whole mass of enormous glass pipes were dangling down into the river from somewhere high up in the ceiling! They really were *enormous,* those pipes. There must have been a dozen of them at least, and they were sucking up the brownish muddy water from the river and carrying it away to goodness knows where. And because they were made of glass, you could see the liquid flowing and bubbling along inside them, and above the noise of the waterfall, you could hear the never-ending suck-suck-sucking sound of the pipes as they did their work.

Graceful trees and bushes were growing along the riverbanks—weeping willows and alders and tall clumps of rhododendrons with their pink and red and mauve blossoms. In the meadows there were thousands of buttercups.

"There!" cried Mr. Wonka, dancing up and down and pointing his gold-topped cane at the great brown river. "It's *all* chocolate! Every drop of that river is hot melted chocolate of the finest quality. The *very* finest quality. There's enough chocolate in there to fill *every* bathtub in the *entire* country! *And* all the swimming pools as well! Isn't it *terrific*? And just look at my pipes! They suck up the chocolate and carry it away to all the other rooms in the factory where it is needed! Thousands of gallons an hour, my dear children! Thousands and thousands of gallons!"

The children and their parents were too flabbergasted to speak. They were staggered. They were dumfounded. They were bewildered and dazzled. They were com-

pletely bowled over by the hugeness of the whole thing. They simply stood and stared.

"The waterfall is *most* important!" Mr. Wonka went on. "It mixes the chocolate! It churns it up! It pounds it and beats it! It makes it light and frothy! No other factory in the world mixes its chocolate by waterfall! But it's the *only* way to do it properly! The *only* way! And do you like my trees?" he cried, pointing with his stick. "And my lovely bushes? Don't you think they look pretty? I told you I hated ugliness! And of course they are *all* eatable! All made of something different and delicious! And do you like my meadows? Do you like my grass and my buttercups? The grass you are standing on, my dear little ones, is made of a new kind of soft, minty sugar that I've just invented! I call it swudge! Try a blade! Please do! It's delectable!"

Automatically, everybody bent down and picked one blade of grass—everybody, that is, except Augustus Gloop, who took a big handful.

And Violet Beauregarde, before tasting her blade of grass, took the piece of world-record-breaking chewing gum out of her mouth and stuck it carefully behind her ear.

"Isn't it *wonderful*!" whispered Charlie. "Hasn't it got a wonderful taste, Grandpa?"

"I could eat the whole *field*!" said Grandpa Joe, grinning with delight. "I could go around on all fours like a cow and eat every blade of grass in the field!"

"Try a buttercup!" cried Mr. Wonka. "They're even *nicer*!"

Suddenly, the air was filled with screams of excitement. The screams came from Veruca Salt. She was pointing frantically to the other side of the river. "*Look*! Look over there!" she screamed. "What *is* it? He's moving! He's walking! It's a little *person*! It's a little *man*! Down there below the waterfall!"

Everybody stopped picking buttercups and stared across the river.

"*She's right, Grandpa!*" cried Charlie. "It *is* a little man! Can you *see* him?"

"I see him, Charlie!" said Grandpa Joe excitedly.

And now everybody started shouting at once.

"There's *two* of them!"

"My gosh, so there is!"

"There's more than two! There's one, two, three, four, five!"

"What are they *doing*?"

"Where do they *come* from?"

"Who *are* they?"

Children and parents alike rushed down to the edge of the river to get a closer look.

"Aren't they *fantastic*!"

"No higher than my knee!"

"Look at their funny long hair!"

The tiny men—they were no larger than medium-sized dolls—had stopped what they were doing, and now they were staring back across the river at the visitors. One of them pointed towards the children, and then he whispered something to the other four, and all five of them burst into peals of laughter.

"But they can't be *real* people," Charlie said.

"Of course they're real people," Mr. Wonka answered. "They're Oompa-Loompas."

16
The Oompa-Loompas

"Oompa-Loompas!" everyone said at once. *"Oompa-Loompas!"*

"Imported direct from Loompaland," said Mr. Wonka proudly.

"There's no such place," said Mrs. Salt.

"Excuse me, dear lady, but . . ."

"Mr. Wonka," cried Mrs. Salt. "I am a teacher of geography . . ."

"Then you'll know all about it," said Mr. Wonka. "And oh, what a terrible country it is! Nothing but thick jungles infested by the most dangerous beasts in the entire world—hornswogglers and snozzwangers and those terrible wicked whangdoodles. A whangdoodle would eat ten Oompa-Loompas for breakfast and come galloping back for a second helping. When I went out there, I found the little Oompa-Loompas living in tree-houses. They *had* to live in tree-houses to escape from the whangdoodles and the hornswogglers and the snozzwangers. And they were practically starving to death. They were living on green caterpillars, and the caterpillars tasted revolting, and the Oompa-Loompas spent every moment of their days climbing through the treetops looking for other things to mash up with the caterpillars to make them taste better—red beetles, for instance, and eucalyptus leaves, and the bark of the bong-bong tree, all of them beastly, but not quite so beastly as the caterpillars. Poor little Oompa-Loompas! The one food that they longed for more than any other was the cacao bean. But they couldn't get it. An Oompa-Loompa was lucky if he found three or four cacao beans a year. But oh, how they craved them. They used to dream about cacao beans all night and talk about them all day. You had only to *mention* the word 'cacao' to an Oompa-Loompa and he would start dribbling at the mouth. The cacao bean," Mr. Wonka continued, "which grows on the cacao tree, happens to be *the thing* from which all chocolate is made. You cannot make chocolate without the cacao bean. The cacao bean *is* chocolate. I myself use billions of cacao beans every week in this factory. And so, my dear children, as soon as

I discovered that the Oompa-Loompas were crazy for this particular food, I climbed up to their tree-house village and poked my head in through the door of the tree house belonging to the leader of the tribe. The poor little fellow, looking thin and starved, was sitting there trying to eat a bowl full of mashed-up green caterpillars without being sick. 'Look here,' I said (speaking not in English, of course, but in Oompa-Loompish), 'look here, if you and all your people will come back to my country and live in my factory, you can have *all* the cacao beans you want! I've got mountains of them in my storehouses! You can have cacao beans for every meal! You can gorge yourselves silly on them! I'll even pay your wages in cacao beans if you wish!'

"'You really mean it?' asked the Oompa-Loompa leader, leaping up from his chair.

"'Of course I mean it,' I said. 'And you can have choco-late as well. Chocolate tastes even better than cacao beans because it's got milk and sugar added.'

"The little man gave a great whoop of joy and threw his bowl of mashed caterpillars right out of the tree-house window. 'It's a deal!' he cried. 'Come on! Let's go!'

"So I shipped them all over here, every man, woman, and child in the Oompa-Loompa tribe. It was easy. I smug-gled them over in large packing cases with holes in them, and they all got here safely. They are wonderful workers. They all speak English now. They love dancing and music. They are always making up songs. I expect you will hear a good deal of singing today from time to time. I must warn you, though, that they are rather mischievous. They like jokes. They still wear the same kind of clothes they wore in the jungle. They insist upon that. The men, as you can see for yourselves across the river, wear only deer-skins. The women wear leaves, and the children wear nothing at all. The women use fresh leaves every day. . . ."

"Daddy!" shouted Veruca Salt (the girl who got every-thing she wanted). *"Daddy!* I want an Oompa-Loompa! I want you to get me an Oompa-Loompa! I want an Oompa-Loompa right away! I want to take it home with me! Go on, Daddy! Get me an Oompa-Loompa!"

"Now, now, my pet!" her father said to her, "we mustn't interrupt Mr. Wonka."

"But I want an Oompa-Loompa!" screamed Veruca.

"All *right,* Veruca, all *right.* But I can't get it for you this second. Please be patient. I'll see you have one before the day is out."

"Augustus!" shouted Mrs. Gloop. "Augustus, sweetheart,

I don't think you had better do *that*." Augustus Gloop, as you might have guessed, had quietly sneaked down to the edge of the river, and he was now kneeling on the river-bank, scooping hot melted chocolate into his mouth as fast as he could.

17
Augustus Gloop Goes up the Pipe

WHEN MR. WONKA turned round and saw what Augustus Gloop was doing, he cried out, "Oh, no! *Please*, Augustus, *please*! I beg of you not to do that. My chocolate must be untouched by human hands!"

"Augustus!" called out Mrs. Gloop. "Didn't you hear what the man said? Come away from that river at once!"

"This stuff is *tee*-riffic!" said Augustus, taking not the slightest notice of his mother or Mr. Wonka. "Oh boy, I need a bucket to drink it properly!"

"Augustus," cried Mr. Wonka, hopping up and down and waggling his stick in the air, "you *must* come away. You are dirtying my chocolate!"

"Augustus!" cried Mrs. Gloop.

"Augustus!" cried Mr. Gloop.

But Augustus was deaf to everything except the call of his enormous stomach. He was now lying full length on the ground with his head far out over the river, lapping up the chocolate like a dog.

"Augustus!" shouted Mrs. Gloop. "You'll be giving that nasty cold of yours to about a million people all over the country!"

"Be careful, Augustus!" shouted Mr. Gloop. "You're leaning too far out!"

Mr. Gloop was absolutely right. For suddenly there was a shriek, and then a splash, and into the river went Augustus Gloop, and in one second he had disappeared under the brown surface.

"Save him!" screamed Mrs. Gloop, going white in the face, and waving her umbrella about. "He'll drown! He can't swim a yard! Save him! Save him!"

"Good heavens, woman," said Mr. Gloop, "I'm not diving in there! I've got my best suit on!"

Augustus Gloop's face came up again to the surface, painted brown with chocolate. "Help! Help! Help!" he yelled. "Fish me out!"

"Don't just *stand* there!" Mrs. Gloop screamed at Mr. Gloop. "*Do* something!"

"I *am* doing something!" said Mr. Gloop, who was now taking off his jacket and getting ready to dive into the chocolate. But while he was doing this, the wretched boy was being sucked closer and closer toward the mouth of one of the great pipes that was dangling down into the river. Then all at once, the powerful suction took hold of him completely, and he was pulled under the surface and then into the mouth of the pipe.

The crowd on the riverbank waited breathlessly to see where he would come out.

"There he goes!" somebody shouted, pointing upwards.

And sure enough, because the pipe was made of glass, Augustus Gloop could be clearly seen shooting up inside it, head first, like a torpedo.

"Help! Murder! Police!" screamed Mrs. Gloop. "Augustus, come back at once! Where are you going?"

"It's a wonder to me," said Mr. Gloop, "how that pipe is big enough for him to go through it."

"It *isn't* big enough!" said Charlie Bucket. "Oh dear, look! He's slowing down!"

"So he is!" said Grandpa Joe.

"He's going to stick!" said Charlie.

"I think he is!" said Grandpa Joe.

"By golly, he *has* stuck!" said Charlie.

"It's his stomach that's done it!" said Mr. Gloop.

"He's blocked the whole pipe!" said Grandpa Joe.

"Smash the pipe!" yelled Mrs. Gloop, still waving her umbrella. "Augustus, come out of there at once!"

The watchers below could see the chocolate swishing around the boy in the pipe, and they could see it building up behind him in a solid mass, pushing against the blockage. The pressure was terrific. Something had to give. Something did give, and that something was Augustus. *WHOOF!* Up he shot again like a bullet in the barrel of a gun.

"He's disappeared!" yelled Mrs. Gloop. "Where does that pipe go to? Quick! Call the fire brigade!"

"Keep calm!" cried Mr. Wonka. "Keep calm, my dear lady, keep calm. There is no danger! No danger whatsoever! Augustus has gone on a little journey, that's all. A most interesting little journey. But he'll come out of it just fine, you wait and see."

"How can he possibly come out just fine!" snapped Mrs. Gloop. "He'll be made into marshmallows in five seconds!"

"Impossible!" cried Mr. Wonka. "Unthinkable! Inconceivable! Absurd! He could never be made into marshmallows!"

"And why not, may I ask?" shouted Mrs. Gloop.

"Because that pipe doesn't *go* to the Marshmallow Room!" Mr. Wonka answered. "It doesn't go anywhere near it! That pipe—the one Augustus went up—happens to lead directly to the room where I make a most delicious kind of strawberry-flavored chocolate-coated fudge. . . ."

"Then he'll be made into strawberry-flavored chocolate-coated fudge!" screamed Mrs. Gloop. "My poor Augustus! They'll be selling him by the pound all over the country tomorrow morning!"

"Quite right," said Mr. Gloop.

"I *know* I'm right," said Mrs. Gloop.

"It's beyond a joke," said Mr. Gloop.

"Mr. Wonka doesn't seem to think so!" cried Mrs. Gloop. "Just look at him! He's laughing his head off! How *dare* you laugh like that when my boy's just gone up the pipe! You monster!" she shrieked, pointing her umbrella at Mr. Wonka as though she were going to run him through. "You think it's a joke, do you? You think that sucking my boy up into your Fudge Room like that is just one great big colossal joke?"

"He'll be perfectly safe," said Mr. Wonka, giggling slightly.

"He'll be chocolate fudge!" shrieked Mrs. Gloop.

"Never!" cried Mr. Wonka.

"Of course he will!" shrieked Mrs. Gloop.

"I wouldn't allow it!" cried Mr. Wonka.

"And why not?" shrieked Mrs. Gloop.

"Because the taste would be terrible," said Mr. Wonka. "Just imagine it! Augustus-flavored chocolate-coated Gloop! No one would buy it."

"They most certainly would!" cried Mr. Gloop indignantly.

"I don't want to think about it!" shrieked Mrs. Gloop.

"Nor do I," said Mr. Wonka. "And I do promise you, madam, that your darling boy is perfectly safe."

"If he's perfectly safe, then where is he?" snapped Mrs. Gloop. "Lead me to him this instant!"

Mr. Wonka turned around and clicked his fingers sharply, *click, click, click,* three times. Immediately, an Oompa-Loompa appeared, as if from nowhere, and stood beside him.

The Oompa-Loompa bowed and smiled, showing beautiful white teeth. His skin was rosy-white, his long hair was golden-brown, and the top of his head came just above the height of Mr. Wonka's knee. He wore the usual deerskin slung over his shoulder.

"Now listen to me!" said Mr. Wonka, looking down at the tiny man, "I want you to take Mr. and Mrs. Gloop up to the Fudge Room and help them to find their son, Augustus. He's just gone up the pipe."

The Oompa-Loompa took one look at Mrs. Gloop and exploded into peals of laughter.

"Oh, do be quiet!" said Mr. Wonka. "Control yourself! Pull yourself together! Mrs. Gloop doesn't think it's at all funny!"

"You can say that again!" said Mrs. Gloop.

"Go straight to the Fudge Room," Mr. Wonka said to the Oompa-Loompa, "and when you get there, take a long stick and start poking around inside the big chocolate-mixing barrel. I'm almost certain you'll find him in there.

But you'd better look sharp! You'll have to hurry! If you leave him in the chocolate-mixing barrel too long, he's liable to get poured out into the fudge boiler, and that really *would* be a disaster, wouldn't it? My fudge would become *quite* uneatable!"

Mrs. Gloop let out a shriek of fury.

"I'm joking," said Mr. Wonka, giggling madly behind his beard. "I didn't mean it. Forgive me. I'm so sorry. Good-by, Mrs. Gloop! And Mr. Gloop! Good-by! Good-by! I'll see you later. . . ."

As Mr. and Mrs. Gloop and their tiny escort hurried away, the five Oompa-Loompas on the far side of the river suddenly began hopping and dancing about and beating wildly upon a number of very small drums. "Augustus Gloop!" they chanted. "Augustus Gloop! Augustus Gloop! Augustus Gloop!"

"Grandpa!" cried Charlie. "Listen to them, Grandpa! What *are* they doing?"

"Ssshh!" whispered Grandpa Joe. "I think they're going to sing us a song!"

"Augustus Gloop!" chanted the Oompa-Loompas.
"Augustus Gloop! Augustus Gloop!
The great big greedy nincompoop!
How long could we allow this beast
To gorge and guzzle, feed and feast
On everything he wanted to?
Great Scott! It simply wouldn't do!
However long this pig might live,
We're positive he'd never give
Even the smallest bit of fun

Or happiness to anyone.
So what we do in cases such
As this, we use the gentle touch,
And carefully we take the brat
And turn him into something that
Will give great pleasure to us all—
A doll, for instance, or a ball,
Or marbles or a rocking horse.
But this revolting boy, of course,
Was so unutterably vile,
So greedy, foul, and infantile,
He left a most disgusting taste
Inside our mouths, and so in haste
We chose a thing that, come what may,
Would take the nasty taste away.
'Come on!' we cried, 'The time is ripe
To send him shooting up the pipe!
He has to go! It has to be!'
And very soon, he's going to see
Inside the room to which he's gone
Some funny things are going on.
But don't, dear children, be alarmed;
Augustus Gloop will not be harmed,
Although, of course, we must admit
He will be altered *quite a bit.*
He'll be quite *changed from what he's been,*
When he goes through the fudge machine:
Slowly, the wheels go round and round,
The cogs begin to grind and pound;
A hundred knives to slice, slice, slice;
We add some sugar, cream, and spice;

We boil him for a minute more,
Until we're absolutely sure
That all the greed and all the gall
Is boiled away for once and all.
Then out he comes! And now! By grace!
A miracle has taken place!
This boy, who only just before
Was loathed by men from shore to shore,
This greedy brute, this louse's ear,
Is loved by people everywhere!
For who could hate or bear a grudge
Against a luscious bit of fudge?"

"I *told* you they loved singing!" cried Mr. Wonka. "Aren't they delightful? Aren't they charming? But you mustn't believe a word they said. It's all nonsense, every bit of it!"

"Are the Oompa-Loompas really joking, Grandpa?" asked Charlie.

"Of course they're joking," answered Grandpa Joe. "They *must* be joking. At least, I hope they're joking. Don't you?"

18
Down the Chocolate River

"OFF WE GO!" cried Mr. Wonka. "Hurry up, everybody! Follow me to the next room! And please don't worry about

Augustus Gloop. He's bound to come out in the wash. They always do. We shall have to make the next part of the journey by boat! Here she comes! Look!"

A steamy mist was rising up now from the great warm chocolate river, and out of the mist there appeared suddenly a most fantastic pink boat. It was a large open rowboat with a tall front and a tall back (like a Viking boat of old), and it was of such a shining sparkling glistening pink color that the whole thing looked as though it were made of bright, pink glass. There were many oars on either side of it, and as the boat came closer, the watchers on the riverbank could see that the oars were being pulled by masses of Oompa-Loompas—at least ten of them to each oar.

"This is my private yacht!" cried Mr. Wonka, beaming with pleasure. "I made her by hollowing out an enormous boiled sweet! Isn't she beautiful! See how she comes cutting through the river!"

The gleaming pink boiled-sweet boat glided up to the riverbank. One hundred Oompa-Loompas rested on their oars and stared up at the visitors. Then suddenly, for some reason best known to themselves, they all burst into shrieks of laughter.

"What's so funny?" asked Violet Beauregarde.

"Oh, don't worry about *them*!" cried Mr. Wonka. "They're always laughing! They think everything's a colossal joke! Jump into the boat, all of you! Come on! Hurry up!"

As soon as everyone was safely in, the Oompa-Loompas pushed the boat away from the bank and began to row swiftly down river.

"Hey, there! Mike Teavee!" shouted Mr. Wonka. "Please

do not lick the boat with your tongue! It'll only make it sticky!"

"Daddy," said Veruca Salt, "I want a boat like this! I want you to buy me a big pink boiled-sweet boat exactly like Mr. Wonka's! And I want lots of Oompa-Loompas to row me about, and I want a chocolate river and I want . . . I want . . ."

"She wants a good kick in the pants," whispered Grandpa Joe to Charlie. The old man was sitting in the back of the boat and little Charlie Bucket was right beside him. Charlie was holding tightly onto his grandfather's bony old hand. He was in a whirl of excitement. Everything that he had seen so far—the great chocolate river, the waterfall, the huge sucking pipes, the candy meadows, the Oompa-Loompas, the beautiful pink boat, and most of all, Mr. Willy Wonka himself—had been so astonishing that he began to wonder whether there could possibly be any more astonishments left. Where were they going now? What were they going to see? And what in the world was going to happen in the next room?

"Isn't it marvelous?" said Grandpa Joe, grinning at Charlie.

Charlie nodded and smiled up at the old man.

Suddenly, Mr. Wonka, who was sitting on Charlie's other side, reached down into the bottom of the boat, picked up a large mug, dipped it into the river, filled it with chocolate, and handed it to Charlie. "Drink this," he said. "It'll do you good! You looked starved to death!"

Then Mr. Wonka filled a second mug and gave it to Grandpa Joe. "You, too," he said. "You look like a skeleton! What's the matter? Hasn't there been anything to eat in your house lately?"

"Not much," said Grandpa Joe.

Charlie put the mug to his lips, and as the rich warm creamy chocolate ran down his throat into his empty tummy, his whole body from head to toe began to tingle with pleasure, and a feeling of intense happiness spread over him.

"You like it?" asked Mr. Wonka.

"Oh, it's wonderful!" Charlie said.

"The creamiest loveliest chocolate I've ever tasted!" said Grandpa Joe, smacking his lips.

"That's because it's been mixed by waterfall," Mr. Wonka told him.

The boat sped on down the river. The river was getting narrower. There was some kind of a dark tunnel ahead—a great round tunnel that looked like an enormous pipe—and the river was running right into the tunnel. And so was the boat! "Row on!" shouted Mr. Wonka, jumping up and waving his stick in the air. "Full speed ahead!" And with the Oompa-Loompas rowing faster than ever, the boat shot into the pitch-dark tunnel, and all the passengers screamed with excitement.

"How can they see where they're going?" shrieked Violet Beauregarde in the darkness.

"There's no knowing where they're going!" cried Mr. Wonka, hooting with laughter.

"There's no earthly way of knowing
Which direction they are going!
There's no knowing where they're rowing,
Or which way the river's flowing!
Not a speck of light is showing,

So the danger must be growing,
For the rowers keep on rowing,
And they're certainly not showing
Any signs that they are slowing...."

"He's gone off his rocker!" shouted one of the fathers, aghast, and the other parents joined in the chorus of frightened shouting. "He's crazy!" they shouted.

"He's balmy!"

"He's nutty!"

"He's screwy!"

"He's batty!"

"He's dippy!"

"He's dotty!"

"He's daffy!"

"He's goofy!"

"He's beany!"

"He's buggy!"

"He's wacky!"

"He's loony!"

"No, he is *not*!" said Grandpa Joe.

"Switch on the lights!" shouted Mr. Wonka. And suddenly, on came the lights and the whole tunnel was brilliantly lit up, and Charlie could see that they were indeed inside a gigantic pipe, and the great upward-curving walls of the pipe were pure white and spotlessly clean. The river of chocolate was flowing very fast inside the pipe, and the Oompa-Loompas were all rowing like crazy, and the boat was rocketing along at a furious pace. Mr. Wonka was jumping up and down in the back of the boat and calling to the rowers to row faster and faster still. He seemed to love the sensation of whizzing through a white tunnel in a pink boat on a chocolate river, and he clapped his hands and laughed and kept glancing at his passengers to see if they were enjoying it as much as he.

"Look, Grandpa!" cried Charlie. "There's a door in the wall!" It was a green door and it was set into the wall of the tunnel just above the level of the river. As they flashed past it there was just enough time to read the writing on the door: STOREROOM NUMBER 54, it said. ALL THE CREAMS—DAIRY CREAM, WHIPPED CREAM, VIOLET CREAM, COFFEE CREAM, PINEAPPLE CREAM, VANILLA CREAM, AND HAIR CREAM.

"Hair cream?" cried Mike Teavee. "You don't use *hair cream*?"

"Row on!" shouted Mr. Wonka. "There's no time to answer silly questions!"

They streaked past a black door. STOREROOM NUMBER 71, it said on it. WHIPS—ALL SHAPES AND SIZES.

"*Whips!*" cried Veruca Salt. "What on earth do you use whips for?"

"For whipping cream, of course," said Mr. Wonka. "How can you whip cream without whips? Whipped cream isn't whipped cream at all unless it's been whipped with whips. Just as a poached egg isn't a poached egg unless it's been stolen from the woods in the dead of night! Row on, please!"

They passed a yellow door on which it said: STOREROOM NUMBER 77—ALL THE BEANS, CACAO BEANS, COFFEE BEANS, JELLY BEANS, AND HAS BEANS.

"*Has beans?*" cried Violet Beauregarde.

"You're one yourself!" said Mr. Wonka. "There's no time

for arguing! Press on, press on!" But five seconds later, when a bright red door came into sight ahead, he suddenly waved his gold-topped cane in the air and shouted, "Stop the boat!"

19

The Inventing Room—Everlasting Gobstoppers and Hair Toffee

WHEN MR. WONKA SHOUTED "Stop the boat!", the Oompa-Loompas jammed their oars into the river and backed water furiously. The boat stopped.

The Oompa-Loompas guided the boat alongside the red door. On the door it said, INVENTING ROOM—PRIVATE—KEEP OUT. Mr. Wonka took a key from his pocket, leaned over the side of the boat, and put the key in the keyhole.

"*This* is the most important room in the entire factory!" he said. "All my most secret new inventions are cooking and simmering in here! Old Fickelgruber would give his front teeth to be allowed inside just for three minutes! So would Prodnose and Slugworth and all the other rotten chocolate makers! But now, listen to me! I want no messing about when you go in! No touching, no meddling, and no tasting! Is that agreed?"

"Yes, yes!" the children cried. "We won't touch a thing!"

"Up to now," Mr. Wonka said, "nobody else, not even an

Oompa-Loompa, has ever been allowed in here!" He opened the door and stepped out of the boat into the room. The four children and their parents all scrambled after him.

"Don't touch!" shouted Mr. Wonka. "And don't knock anything over!"

Charlie Bucket stared around the gigantic room in which he now found himself. The place was like a witch's kitchen! All about him black metal pots were boiling and bubbling on huge stoves, and kettles were hissing and pans were sizzling, and strange iron machines were clanking and spluttering, and there were pipes running all over the ceiling and walls, and the whole place was filled with smoke and steam and delicious rich smells.

Mr. Wonka himself had suddenly become even more excited than usual, and anyone could see that this was the room he loved best of all. He was hopping about among the saucepans and the machines like a child among his Christmas presents, not knowing which thing to look at first. He lifted the lid from a huge pot and took a sniff; then he rushed over and dipped a finger into a barrel of sticky yellow stuff and had a taste; then he skipped across to one of the machines and turned half a dozen knobs this way and that; then he peered anxiously through the glass door of a gigantic oven, rubbing his hands and cackling with delight at what he saw inside. Then he ran over to another machine, a small shiny affair that kept going *phut-phut-phut-phut-phut,* and every time it went *phut,* a large green marble dropped out of it into a basket on the floor. At least it looked like a marble.

"Everlasting Gobstoppers!" cried Mr. Wonka proudly.

"They're completely new! I am inventing them for children who are given very little pocket money. You can put an Everlasting Gobstopper in your mouth and you can suck it and suck it and suck it and suck it and suck it and it will *never* get any smaller!"

"It's like gum!" cried Violet Beauregarde.

"It is *not* like gum," Mr. Wonka said. "Gum is for chewing, and if you tried chewing one of these Gobstoppers here you'd break your teeth off. But they taste terrific! And they change color once a week! And they *never* get any smaller! They *never* disappear! *NEVER!* At least I don't think they do. There's one of them being tested this very moment in the Testing Room next door. An Oompa-Loompa is sucking it. He's been sucking it for very nearly a year now without stopping, and it's still just as good as ever!

"Now, over here," Mr. Wonka went on, skipping excitedly across the room to the opposite wall, "over here I am inventing a completely new line in toffees!" He stopped beside a large saucepan. The saucepan was full of thick gooey purplish treacle, boiling and bubbling. By standing on his toes, little Charlie could just see inside it.

"That's Hair Toffee!" cried Mr. Wonka. "You eat just one tiny bit of that, and in exactly half an hour a brand-new luscious thick silky beautiful crop of hair will start growing out all over the top of your head! And a moustache! And a beard!"

"A beard!" cried Veruca Salt. "Who wants a beard, for heaven's sake?"

"It would suit you very well," said Mr. Wonka, "but unfortunately the mixture is not quite right yet. I've got it too strong. It works too well. I tried it on an Oompa-

Loompa yesterday in the Testing Room and immediately a huge beard started shooting out of his chin, and the beard grew so fast that soon it was trailing all over the floor in a thick hairy carpet. It was growing faster than we could cut it! In the end we had to use a lawn mower to keep it in check! But I'll get the mixture right soon! And when I do, then there'll be no excuse any more for little boys and girls going about with bald heads!"

"But Mr. Wonka," said Mike Teavee, "little boys and girls never *do* go about with . . ."

"Don't argue, my dear child, *please* don't argue!" cried Mr. Wonka. "It's such a waste of precious time! Now, over *here*, if you will all step this way, I will show you something that I am terrifically proud of. Oh, do be careful! Don't knock anything over! Stand back!"

20
The Great Gum Machine

MR. WONKA LED THE PARTY over to a gigantic machine that stood in the very center of the Inventing Room. It was a mountain of gleaming metal that towered high above the children and their parents. Out of the very top of it there sprouted hundreds and hundreds of thin glass tubes, and the glass tubes all curled downwards and came together in a bunch and hung suspended over an enormous round tub as big as a bath.

"Here we go!" cried Mr. Wonka, and he pressed three different buttons on the side of the machine. A second later, a mighty rumbling sound came from inside it, and the whole machine began to shake most frighteningly, and steam began hissing out of it all over, and then suddenly the watchers noticed that runny stuff was pouring down the insides of all the hundreds of little glass tubes and squirting out into the great tub below. And in every single tube the runny stuff was of a different color, so that all the colors of the rainbow (and many others as well) came sloshing and splashing into the tub. It was a lovely sight. And when the tub was nearly full, Mr. Wonka pressed another button, and immediately the runny stuff stopped running out of the tubes, the rumbling sound disappeared, and a whizzing whirring noise took its place; and then a giant whizzer started whizzing round inside the enormous tub, mixing up all the different colored liquids like an ice-cream soda. Gradually, the mixture began to froth. It became frothier and frothier, and it turned from blue to white to green to brown to yellow, then back to blue again.

"Watch!" said Mr. Wonka.

Click went the machine, and the whizzer stopped whizzing. And now there came a sort of sucking noise, and very quickly all the blue frothy mixture in the huge basin was sucked back into the stomach of the machine. There was a moment of silence. Then a few queer rumblings were heard. Then silence again. Then suddenly, the machine let out a monstrous mighty groan, and at the same moment a tiny drawer (no bigger than the drawer in a slot machine) popped out of the side of the machine, and in the drawer there lay something so small and thin and grey that everyone thought it must be a mistake. The thing looked like a little strip of grey cardboard.

The children and their parents stared at the little grey strip lying in the drawer.

"You mean that's *all*?" said Mike Teavee, disgusted.

"That's all," answered Mr. Wonka, gazing proudly at the result. "Don't you know what it is?"

There was a pause. Then suddenly, Violet Beauregarde,

the goofy gum-chewing girl, let out a yell of excitement. "By gum, it's *gum*!" she shrieked. "It's a stick of chewing gum!"

"Right you are!" cried Mr. Wonka, slapping Violet hard on the back. "It's a stick of gum! It's a stick of the most *amazing* and *fabulous* and *sensational* gum in the world!"

21
Good-by Violet

"THIS GUM," Mr. Wonka went on, "is my latest, my greatest, my most fascinating invention! It's a chewing-gum meal! It's . . . it's . . . it's . . . that tiny little strip of gum lying there is a whole three-course dinner all by itself!"

"What sort of nonsense is this?" said one of the fathers.

"My dear sir!" cried Mr. Wonka. "When I start selling this gum in the shops it will change *everything*! It will be the end of all kitchens and all cooking! There will be no more marketing to do! No more buying of meat and groceries! There'll be no knives and forks at mealtimes! No plates! No washing up! No garbage! No mess! Just a little strip of Wonka's magic chewing gum—and that's all you'll ever need at breakfast, lunch, and supper! This piece of gum I've just made happens to be tomato soup, roast beef, and blueberry pie, but you can have almost anything you want!"

"What *do* you mean, it's tomato soup, roast beef, and blueberry pie?" said Violet Beauregarde.

"If you were to start chewing it," said Mr. Wonka, "then that is exactly what you would get on the menu. It's absolutely amazing! You can actually *feel* the food going down your throat and into your tummy! And you can taste it perfectly! And it fills you up! It satisfies you! It's terrific!"

"It's utterly impossible," said Veruca Salt.

"Just so long as it's gum," shouted Violet Beauregarde, "just so long as it's a piece of gum and I can chew it, then *that's* for me!" And quickly she took her own world-record piece of chewing gum out of her mouth and stuck it behind her left ear. "Come on, Mr. Wonka," she said, "hand over this magic gum of yours and we'll see if the thing works."

"Now, Violet," said Mrs. Beauregarde, her mother, "don't let's do anything silly, Violet."

"I want the gum!" Violet said obstinately. "What's so silly?"

"I would rather you didn't take it," Mr. Wonka told her gently. "You see, I haven't got it *quite right* yet. There are still one or two things. . . ."

"Oh, to heck with that!" said Violet, and suddenly, before Mr. Wonka could stop her, she shot out a fat hand and grabbed the stick of gum out of the little drawer and popped it into her mouth. At once, her huge well-trained jaws started chewing away on it like a pair of tongs.

"Don't!" said Mr. Wonka.

"Fabulous!" shouted Violet. "It's tomato soup! It's hot and creamy and delicious! I can feel it running down my throat!"

"Stop!" said Mr. Wonka. "The gum isn't ready yet! It's not right!"

"Of course it's right!" said Violet. "It's working beautifully! Oh my, what lovely soup this is!"

"Spit it out!" said Mr. Wonka.

"It's changing!" shouted Violet, chewing and grinning both at the same time. "The second course is coming up! It's roast beef! It's tender and juicy! Oh boy, what a flavor! The baked potato is marvelous, too! It's got a crispy skin and it's all filled with butter inside!"

"But how *in*-teresting, Violet," said Mrs. Beauregarde. "You *are* a clever girl."

"Keep chewing, kiddo!" said Mr. Beauregarde. "Keep right on chewing, baby! This is a great day for the Beauregardes! Our little girl is the first person in the world to have a chewing-gum meal!"

Everybody was watching Violet Beauregarde as she stood there chewing this extraordinary gum. Little Charlie Bucket was staring at her absolutely spellbound, watching her huge rubbery lips as they pressed and unpressed with the chewing, and Grandpa Joe stood beside him, gaping at the girl. Mr. Wonka was wringing his hands and saying, "No, no, no, no, no! It isn't ready for eating! It isn't right! You mustn't do it!"

"Blueberry pie and cream!" shouted Violet. "Here it comes! Oh my, it's perfect! It's beautiful! It's . . . it's exactly as though I'm swallowing it! It's as though I'm chewing and swallowing great big spoonfuls of the most marvelous blueberry pie in the world!"

"Good heavens, girl!" shrieked Mrs. Beauregarde suddenly, staring at Violet, "what's happening to your nose!"

"Oh, be quiet, mother, and let me finish!" said Violet.

"It's turning blue!" screamed Mrs. Beauregarde. "Your nose is turning blue as a blueberry!"

"Your mother is right!" shouted Mr. Beauregarde. "Your whole nose has gone purple!"

"What *do* you mean?" said Violet, still chewing away.

"Your cheeks!" screamed Mrs. Beauregarde. "They're turning blue as well! So is your chin! Your whole face is turning blue!"

"Spit that gum out at once!" ordered Mr. Beauregarde.

"Mercy! Save us!" yelled Mrs. Beauregarde. "The girl's going blue and purple all over! Even her hair is changing color! Violet, you're turning violet, Violet! What *is* happening to you!"

"I *told* you I hadn't got it quite right," sighed Mr. Wonka, shaking his head sadly.

"I'll say you haven't!" cried Mrs. Beauregarde. "Just look at the girl now!"

Everybody was staring at Violet. And what a terrible peculiar sight she was! Her face and hands and legs and neck, in fact the skin all over her body, as well as her great big mop of curly hair, had turned a brilliant, purplish-blue, the color of blueberry juice!

"It *always* goes wrong when we come to the dessert," sighed Mr. Wonka. "It's the blueberry pie that does it. But I'll get it right one day, you wait and see."

"Violet," screamed Mrs. Beauregarde, "you're swelling up!"

"I feel sick," Violet said.

"You're swelling up!" screamed Mrs. Beauregarde again.

"I feel most peculiar!" gasped Violet.

"I'm not surprised!" said Mr. Beauregarde.

"Great heavens, girl!" screeched Mrs. Beauregarde. "You're blowing up like a balloon!"

"Like a blueberry," said Mr. Wonka.

"Call a doctor!" shouted Mr. Beauregarde.

"Prick her with a pin!" said one of the other fathers.

"Save her!" cried Mrs. Beauregarde, wringing her hands.

But there was no saving her now. Her body was swelling up and changing shape at such a rate that within a minute it had turned into nothing less than an enormous round blue ball—a gigantic blueberry, in fact—and all that remained of Violet Beauregarde herself was a tiny pair of legs and a tiny pair of arms sticking out of the great round fruit and a little head on top.

"It *always* happens like that," sighed Mr. Wonka. "I've tried it twenty times in the Testing Room on twenty Oompa-Loompas, and every one of them finished up as a blueberry. It's most annoying. I just can't understand it."

"But I don't want a blueberry for a daughter!" yelled Mrs. Beauregarde. "Put her back to what she was this instant!"

Mr. Wonka clicked his fingers, and ten Oompa-Loompas appeared immediately at his side.

"Roll Miss Beauregarde into the boat," he said to them, "and take her along to the Juicing Room at once."

"The *Juicing Room*?" cried Mrs. Beauregarde. "What are they going to do to her there?"

"Squeeze her," said Mr. Wonka. "We've got to squeeze the juice out of her immediately. After that, we'll just have to see how she comes out. But don't worry, my dear Mrs. Beauregarde. We'll get her repaired if it's the last thing we do. I *am* sorry about it all, I really am. . . ."

Already the ten Oompa-Loompas were rolling the enormous blueberry across the floor of the Inventing Room toward the door that led to the chocolate river where the boat was waiting. Mr. and Mrs. Beauregarde hurried after them. The rest of the party, including little Charlie Bucket and Grandpa Joe, stood absolutely still and watched them go.

"Listen!" whispered Charlie. "Listen, Grandpa! The Oompa-Loompas in the boat outside are starting to sing!"

The voices, one hundred of them singing together, came loud and clear into the room:

> *"Dear friends, we surely all agree*
> *There's almost nothing worse to see*
> *Than some repulsive little bum*
> *Who's always chewing chewing gum.*
> *(It's very near as bad as those*

Who sit around and pick the nose).
So please believe us when we say
That chewing gum will never pay;
This sticky habit's bound to send
The chewer to a sticky end.
Did any of you ever know
A person called Miss Bigelow?
This dreadful woman saw no wrong
In chewing, chewing all day long.
She chewed while bathing in the tub,
She chewed while dancing at her club,
She chewed in church and on the bus;
It really was quite ludicrous!
And when she couldn't find her gum,
She'd chew up the linoleum,
Or anything that happened near—
A pair of boots, the postman's ear,
Or other people's underclothes,
And once she chewed her boy friend's nose.
She went on chewing till, at last,
Her chewing muscles grew so vast
That from her face her giant chin
Stuck out just like a violin.
For years and years she chewed away,
Consuming fifty packs a day,
Until one summer's eve, alas,
A horrid business came to pass.
Miss Bigelow went late to bed,
For half an hour she lay and read,
Chewing and chewing all the while
Like some great clockwork crocodile.

At last, she put her gum away
Upon a special little tray,
And settled back and went to sleep—
(She managed this by counting sheep).
But now, how strange! Although she slept,
Those massive jaws of hers still kept
On chewing, chewing through the night,
Even with nothing there to bite.
They were, you see, in such a groove
They positively had *to move.*
And very grim it was to hear
In pitch darkness, loud and clear,
This sleeping woman's great big trap
Opening and shutting, snap-snap-snap!
Faster and faster, chop-chop-chop,
The noise went on, it wouldn't stop.
Until at last her jaws decide

To pause and open extra wide,
And with the most tremendous chew
They bit the lady's tongue in two.
Thereafter, just from chewing gum,
Miss Bigelow was always dumb,
And spent her life shut up in some
Disgusting sanatorium.
And that is why we'll try so hard
To save Miss Violet Beauregarde
From suffering an equal fate.
She's still quite young. It's not too late,
Provided she survives the cure.
We hope she does. We can't be sure."

22

Along the Corridor

"WELL, WELL, WELL," sighed Mr. Willy Wonka, "two naughty little children gone. Three good little children left. I think we'd better get out of this room quickly before we lose anyone else!"

"But Mr. Wonka," said Charlie Bucket anxiously, "will Violet Beauregarde *ever* be all right again or will she always be a blueberry?"

"They'll de-juice her in no time flat!" declared Mr. Wonka. "They'll roll her into the de-juicing machine, and she'll come out just as thin as a whistle!"

"But will she still be blue all over?" asked Charlie.

"She'll be *purple*!" cried Mr. Wonka. "A fine rich purple from head to toe! But there you are! That's what comes from chewing disgusting gum all day long!"

"If you think gum is so disgusting," said Mike Teavee, "then why do you make it in your factory?"

"I do wish you wouldn't mumble," said Mr. Wonka. "I can't hear a word you're saying. Come on! Off we go! Hurry up! Follow me! We're going into the corridors again!" And so saying, Mr. Wonka scuttled across to the far end of the Inventing Room and went out through a small secret door hidden behind a lot of pipes and stoves. The three remaining children—Veruca Salt, Mike Teavee, and Charlie Bucket—together with the five remaining grownups, followed after him.

Charlie Bucket saw that they were now back in one of

those long pink corridors with many other pink corridors leading out of it. Mr. Wonka was rushing along in front, turning left and right and right and left, and Grandpa Joe was saying, "Keep a good hold of my hand, Charlie. It would be terrible to get lost in here."

Mr. Wonka was saying, "No time for any more messing about! We'll never get *anywhere* at the rate we've been going!" And on he rushed, down the endless pink corridors, with his black top hat perched on the top of his head and his plum-colored velvet coattails flying out behind him like a flag in the wind.

They passed another door, then another and another. There were doors every twenty paces or so along the corridor now, and they all had something written on them, and strange clanking noises were coming from behind several of them, and delicious smells came wafting through the keyholes, and sometimes little jets of colored steam shot out from the cracks underneath.

Grandpa Joe and Charlie were half running and half walking to keep up with Mr. Wonka, but they were able to read what it said on quite a few of the doors as they hurried by. EATABLE MARSHMALLOW PILLOWS, it said on one.

"Marshmallow pillows are terrific!" shouted Mr. Wonka as he dashed by. "They'll be all the rage when I get them into the shops! No time to go in, though! No time to go in!"

LICKABLE WALLPAPER FOR NURSERIES, it said on the next door.

"Lovely stuff, lickable wallpaper!" cried Mr. Wonka, rushing past. "It has pictures of fruits on it—bananas, apples, oranges, grapes, pineapples, strawberries, and snozzberries. . . ."

"*Snozzberries?*" said Mike Teavee.

"Don't interrupt!" said Mr. Wonka. "The wallpaper has pictures of all these fruits printed on it, and when you lick the picture of a banana, it tastes of banana. When you lick a strawberry, it tastes of strawberry. And when you lick a snozzberry, it tastes just exactly like a snozzberry. . . ."

"But what *does* a snozzberry taste like?"

"You're mumbling again," said Mr. Wonka. "Speak louder next time. On we go! Hurry up!"

HOT ICE CREAMS FOR COLD DAYS, it said on the next door.

"*Extremely* useful in the winter," said Mr. Wonka, rushing on. "Hot ice cream warms you up no end in freezing weather. I also make hot ice cubes for putting in hot drinks. Hot ice cubes make hot drinks hotter."

COWS THAT GIVE CHOCOLATE MILK, it said on the next door.

"Ah, my pretty little cows!" cried Mr. Wonka. "How I love those cows!"

"But why can't we *see* them?" asked Veruca Salt. "Why do we have to go rushing on past all these lovely rooms?"

"We shall stop in time!" called out Mr. Wonka. "Don't be so madly impatient!"

FIZZY LIFTING DRINKS, it said on the next door.

"Oh, those are fabulous!" cried Mr. Wonka. "They fill you with bubbles, and the bubbles are full of a special kind of gas, and this gas is so terrifically *lifting* that it lifts you right off the ground just like a balloon, and up you go until your head hits the ceiling—and there you stay."

"But how do you come down again?" asked little Charlie.

"You do a burp, of course," said Mr. Wonka. "You do a great big long rude burp, and *up* comes the gas and *down* comes you! But don't drink it outdoors! There's no knowing how high up you'll be carried if you do that. I gave some to an old Oompa-Loompa once out in the back yard and he went up and up and up and disappeared out of sight! It was very sad. I never saw him again."

"He should have burped," Charlie said.

"Of course he should have burped," said Mr. Wonka. "I stood there shouting, 'Burp, you silly ass, burp, or you'll never come down again! But he didn't or couldn't or wouldn't, I don't know which. Maybe he was too polite. He must be on the moon by now."

On the next door, it said, SQUARE CANDIES THAT LOOK ROUND.

"Wait!" cried Mr. Wonka, skidding suddenly to a halt. "I am very proud of my square candies that look round. Let's take a peek."

23
Square Candies That Look Round

EVERYBODY STOPPED and crowded to the door. The top half of the door was made of glass. Grandpa Joe lifted Charlie up so that he could get a better view, and looking in, Charlie saw a long table, and on the table there were rows and rows of small white square-shaped candies. The candies looked very much like square sugar lumps—except that each of them had a funny little pink face painted on one side. At the end of the table, a number of Oompa-Loompas were busily painting more faces on more candies.

"There you are!" cried Mr. Wonka. "Square candies that look round!"

"They don't look round to me," said Mike Teavee.

"They look square," said Veruca Salt. "They look completely square."

"But they *are* square," said Mr. Wonka. "I never said they weren't."

"You said they were *round*!" said Veruca Salt.

"I never said anything of the sort," said Mr. Wonka. "I said they *looked* round."

"But they *don't* look round!" said Veruca Salt. "They look square!"

"They look round," insisted Mr. Wonka.

"They most certainly do not look round!" cried Veruca Salt.

"Veruca, darling," said Mrs. Salt, "pay no attention to Mr. Wonka! He's lying to you!"

"My dear old fish," said Mr. Wonka, "go and boil your head!"

"How dare you speak to me like that!" shouted Mrs. Salt.

"Oh, do shut up," said Mr. Wonka. "Now watch this!" He took a key from his pocket, and unlocked the door, and flung it open . . . and suddenly . . . at the sound of the door opening, all the rows and rows of little square candies looked quickly round to see who was coming in. The tiny faces actually turned toward the door and stared at Mr. Wonka.

"There you are!" he cried triumphantly. "They're looking round! There's no argument about it! They are square
candies that look round!"

"By golly, he's right!" said Grandpa Joe.

"Come on!" said Mr. Wonka, starting off down the corridor again. "On we go! We mustn't dawdle!"

BUTTERSCOTCH AND BUTTERGIN, it said on the next door
they passed.

"Now *that* sounds a bit more interesting," said Mr. Salt,
Veruca's father.

"Glorious stuff!" said Mr. Wonka. "The Oompa-Loompas
all adore it. It makes them tiddly. Listen! You can hear
them in there now, whooping it up."

Shrieks of laughter and snatches of singing could be
heard coming through the closed door.

"They're drunk as lords," said Mr. Wonka. "They're
drinking butterscotch and soda. They like that best of all.

Buttergin and tonic is also very popular. Follow me, please! We really mustn't keep stopping like this." He turned left. He turned right. They came to a long flight of stairs. Mr. Wonka slid down the bannisters. The three children did the same. Mrs. Salt and Mrs. Teavee, the only women now left in the party, were getting very out of breath. Mrs. Salt was a great fat creature with short legs, and she was blowing like a rhinoceros. "This way!" cried Mr. Wonka, turning left at the bottom of the stairs.

"Go *slower*!" panted Mrs. Salt.

"Impossible," said Mr. Wonka. "We should never get there in time if I did."

"Get where?" asked Veruca Salt.

"Never you mind," said Mr. Wonka. "You just wait and see."

24

Veruca in the Nut Room

MR. WONKA RUSHED ON down the corridor. THE NUT ROOM, it said on the next door they came to.

"All right," said Mr. Wonka, "stop here for a moment and catch your breath, and take a peek through the glass panel of this door. But don't go in! Whatever you do, don't go into THE NUT ROOM! If you go in, you'll disturb the squirrels!"

Everyone crowded around the door.

"Oh look, Grandpa, look!" cried Charlie.

"Squirrels!" shouted Veruca Salt.

"Jeepers!" said Mike Teavee.

It was an amazing sight. One hundred squirrels were seated upon high stools around a large table. On the table, there were mounds and mounds of walnuts, and the squirrels were all working away like mad, shelling the walnuts at a tremendous speed.

"These squirrels are specially trained for getting the nuts out of walnuts," Mr. Wonka explained.

"Why use squirrels?" Mike Teavee asked. "Why not use Oompa-Loompas?"

"Because," said Mr. Wonka, "Oompa-Loompas can't get walnuts out of walnut shells in one piece. They always break them in two. Nobody except squirrels can get walnuts *whole* out of walnut shells every time. It is extremely difficult. But in my factory, I insist upon using only whole walnuts. Therefore I have to have squirrels to do the job. Aren't they wonderful, the way they get those nuts out! And see how they first tap each walnut with their knuckles to be sure it's not a bad one! If it's bad, it makes a hollow sound, and they don't bother to open it. They just throw it down the garbage chute. There! Look! Watch that squirrel nearest to us! I think he's got a bad one now!"

They watched the little squirrel as he tapped the walnut shell with his knuckles. He cocked his head to one side, listening intently, then suddenly he threw the nut over his shoulder into a large hole in the floor.

"Hey, Mummy!" shouted Veruca Salt suddenly, "I've decided I want a squirrel! Get me one of those squirrels!"

"Don't be silly, sweetheart," said Mrs. Salt. "These all belong to Mr. Wonka."

"I don't care about that!" shouted Veruca. "I want one. All I've *got* at home is two dogs and four cats and six bunny rabbits and two parakeets and three canaries and a green parrot and a turtle and a bowl of goldfish and a cage of white mice and a silly old hamster! I want a *squirrel*!"

"All right, my pet," Mrs. Salt said soothingly. "Mummy'll get you a squirrel just as soon as she possibly can."

"But I don't want *any* old squirrel!" Veruca shouted. "I want a *trained* squirrel!"

At this point, Mr. Salt, Veruca's father, stepped forward. "Very well, Wonka," he said importantly, taking out a wallet full of money, "how much d'you want for one of these crazy squirrels? Name your price."

"They're not for sale," Mr. Wonka answered. "She can't have one."

"Who says I can't!" shouted Veruca. "I'm going in to grab me a squirrel this very minute!"

"Don't!" said Mr. Wonka quickly, but he was too late. The girl had already thrown open the door and rushed in.

The moment she entered the room, one hundred squirrels stopped what they were doing and turned their heads and stared at her with small black beady eyes.

Veruca Salt stopped also, and stared back at them.

Then her gaze fell upon a pretty little squirrel sitting nearest to her at the end of the table. The squirrel was holding a walnut in its paws.

"All right," Veruca said, "I'll have *you*!"

She reached out her hands to grab the squirrel . . . but as she did so . . . in that first split second when her hands started to go forward, there was a sudden flash of movement in the room, like a flash of brown lightning, and every single squirrel around the table took a flying leap towards her and landed on her body.

Twenty-five of them caught hold of her right arm, and pinned it down.

Twenty-five more caught hold of her left arm, and pinned that down.

Twenty-five caught hold of her right leg and anchored it to the ground.

Twenty-*four* caught hold of her left leg.

And the one remaining squirrel (obviously the leader of them all) climbed up on to her shoulder and started tap-tap-tapping the wretched girl's head with its knuckles.

"Save her!" screamed Mrs. Salt. "Veruca! Come back! What are they *doing* to her?"

"They're testing her to see if she's a bad nut," said Mr. Wonka. "You watch."

Veruca struggled furiously, but the squirrels held her tight and she couldn't move. The squirrel on her shoulder went tap-tap-tapping the side of her head with his knuckles.

Then all at once, the squirrels pulled Veruca to the ground and started carrying her across the floor.

"My goodness, she *is* a bad nut after all," said Mr. Wonka. "Her head must have sounded quite hollow."

Veruca kicked and screamed, but it was no use. The tiny strong paws held her tightly and she couldn't escape.

"Where are they taking her?" shrieked Mrs. Salt.

"She's going where all the other bad nuts go," said Mr. Willy Wonka. "Down the garbage chute."

"By golly, she *is* going down the chute!" said Mr. Salt, staring through the glass door at his daughter.

"Then save her!" cried Mrs. Salt.

"Too late," said Mr. Wonka. "She's gone!"

And indeed she had.

"But where?" shrieked Mrs. Salt, flapping her arms. "What happens to the bad nuts? Where does the chute go to?"

"That *particular* chute," Mr. Wonka told her, "runs directly into the great big main garbage pipe which carries away all the rubbish from every part of the factory— all the floor sweepings and potato peelings and rotten cabbages and fish heads and stuff like that."

"Who eats fish and cabbage and potatoes in *this* factory, I'd like to know?" said Mike Teavee.

"I do, of course," answered Mr. Wonka. "You don't think *I* live on cacao beans, do you?"

"But . . . but . . . but . . ." shrieked Mrs. Salt, "where does the great big pipe go to in the end?"

"Why, to the furnace, of course," Mr. Wonka said calmly. "To the incinerator."

Mrs. Salt opened her huge red mouth and started to scream.

"Don't worry," said Mr. Wonka, "there's always a chance that they've decided not to light it today."

"A *chance*!" yelled Mrs. Salt. "My darling Veruca! She'll . . . she'll . . . she'll be sizzled like a sausage!"

"Quite right, my dear," said Mr. Salt. "Now see here, Wonka," he added, "I think you've gone *just* a shade too far this time, I do indeed. My daughter may be a bit of a frump—I don't mind admitting it—but that doesn't mean you can roast her to a crisp. I'll have you know I'm extremely cross about this, I really am."

"Oh, don't be cross, my dear sir!" said Mr. Wonka. "I expect she'll turn up again sooner or later. She may not even have gone down at all. She may be stuck in the chute just below the entrance hole, and if *that's* the case, all you'll have to do is go in and pull her up again."

Hearing this, both Mr. and Mrs. Salt dashed into the Nut Room and ran over to the hole in the floor and peered in.

"Veruca!" shouted Mrs. Salt. "Are you down there!"

There was no answer.

Mrs. Salt bent further forward to get a closer look. She was now kneeling right on the edge of the hole with her head down and her enormous behind sticking up in the air like a giant mushroom. It was a dangerous position to be in. She needed only one tiny little push . . . one gentle nudge in the right place . . . and *that* is exactly what the squirrels gave her!

Over she toppled, into the hole head first, screeching like a parrot.

"Good gracious me!" said Mr. Salt as he watched his fat wife go tumbling down the hole, "*what* a lot of garbage there's going to be today!" He saw her disappearing into the darkness. "What's it like down there, Angina?" he called out. He leaned further forward.

The squirrels rushed up behind him. . . .

"Help!" he shouted.

But he was already toppling forward, and down the chute he went, just as his wife had done before him—and his daughter.

"Oh *dear*!" cried Charlie, who was watching with the others through the door, "what on earth's going to happen to them now?"

"I expect someone will catch them at the bottom of the chute," said Mr. Wonka.

"But what about the great fiery incinerator?" asked Charlie.

"They only light it every other day," said Mr. Wonka. "Perhaps this is one of the days when they let it go out. You never know . . . they might be lucky. . . ."

"Ssshh!" said Grandpa Joe. "Listen! Here comes another song!"

From far away down the corridor came the beating of drums. Then the singing began.

> *"Veruca Salt!"* sang the Oompa-Loompas.
> *"Veruca Salt, the little brute,*
>   *Has just gone down the garbage chute,*
>   *(And as we very rightly thought*
>   *That in a case like this we ought*
>   *To see the thing completely through,*
>   *We've polished off her parents, too.)*
>   *Down goes Veruca! Down the drain!*
>   *And here, perhaps, we should explain*
>   *That she will meet, as she descends,*
>   *A rather different set of friends*

To those that she has left behind—
These *won't be nearly so refined.*
A fish head, for example, cut
This morning from a halibut.
'Hello! Good morning! How d'you do?
How nice to meet you! How are you?'
And then a little further down
A mass of others gather round:
A bacon rind, some rancid lard,
A loaf of bread gone stale and hard,
A steak that nobody could chew,
An oyster from an oyster stew,
Some liverwurst so old and gray
One smelled it from a mile away,
A rotten nut, a reeky pear,
A thing the cat left on the stair,
And lots of other things as well,
Each with a rather horrid smell.
These *are Veruca's new found friends*
That she will meet as she descends,
And this *is the price she has to pay*
For going so very far astray.
But now, my dears, we think you might
Be wondering—is it really right
That every single bit of blame
And all the scolding and the shame
Should fall upon Veruca Salt?
Is *she* the only one at fault?*
For though she's spoiled, and dreadfully so,
A girl can't spoil herself, you know.
Who *spoiled her, then? Ah, who indeed?*

Who pandered to her every need?
Who turned her into such a brat?
Who are the culprits? Who did that?
Alas! You needn't look so far
To find out who these sinners are.
They are (and this is very sad)
Her loving parents, MUM and DAD.
And that is why we're glad they fell
Into the garbage chute as well.

25

The Great Glass Elevator

"I'VE NEVER SEEN anything like it!" cried Mr. Wonka. "The children are disappearing like rabbits! But you mustn't worry about it! They'll *all* come out in the wash!"

Mr. Wonka looked at the little group that stood beside him in the corridor. There were only two children left now—Mike Teavee and Charlie Bucket. And there were three grownups, Mr. and Mrs. Teavee and Grandpa Joe. "Shall we move on?" Mr. Wonka asked.

"Oh, yes!" cried Charlie and Grandpa Joe, both together.

"My feet are getting tired," said Mike Teavee. "I want to watch television."

"If you're tired then we'd better take the elevator," said Mr. Wonka. "It's over here. Come on! In we go!" He skipped across the passage to a pair of double doors. The doors slid open. The two children and the grownups went in.

"Now then," cried Mr. Wonka, "which button shall we press first? Take your pick!"

Charlie Bucket stared around him in astonishment. This was the craziest elevator he had ever seen. There were buttons everywhere! The walls, and even the *ceiling,* were covered all over with rows and rows and rows of small, black push buttons! There must have been a thousand of them on each wall, and another thousand on the ceiling! And now Charlie noticed that every single button had a tiny printed label beside it telling you which room you would be taken to if you pressed it.

"This isn't just an ordinary up-and-down elevator!" announced Mr. Wonka proudly. "This elevator can go sideways and longways and slantways and any other way you can think of! It can visit any single room in the whole factory, no matter where it is! You simply press the button . . . and *zing*! . . . you're off!"

"*Fantastic*!" murmured Grandpa Joe. His eyes were shining with excitement as he stared at the rows and rows of buttons.

"The whole elevator is made of thick, clear glass!" Mr. Wonka declared. "Walls, doors, ceiling, floor, everything is made of glass so that you can see out!"

"But there's nothing to see," said Mike Teavee.

"Choose a button!" said Mr. Wonka. "The two children may press one button each. So take your pick! Hurry up! In every room, something delicious and wonderful is being made."

Quickly, Charlie started reading some of the labels alongside the buttons.

THE ROCK-CANDY MINE—10,000 FEET DEEP, it said on one.

COKERNUT-ICE SKATING RINKS, it said on another.

Then . . . STRAWBERRY-JUICE WATER PISTOLS.

TOFFEE-APPLE TREES FOR PLANTING OUT IN YOUR GARDEN—ALL SIZES.

EXPLODING CANDY FOR YOUR ENEMIES.

LUMINOUS LOLLIES FOR EATING IN BED AT NIGHT.

MINT JUJUBES FOR THE BOY NEXT DOOR—THEY'LL GIVE HIM GREEN TEETH FOR A MONTH.

CAVITY-FILLING CARAMELS—NO MORE DENTISTS.

STICKJAW FOR TALKATIVE PARENTS.

WRIGGLE-SWEETS THAT WRIGGLE DELIGHTFULLY IN YOUR TUMMY AFTER SWALLOWING.

INVISIBLE CHOCOLATE BARS FOR EATING IN CLASS.

CANDY-COATED PENCILS FOR SUCKING.

FIZZY LEMONADE SWIMMING POOLS.

MAGIC HAND-FUDGE—WHEN YOU HOLD IT IN YOUR HAND, YOU TASTE IT IN YOUR MOUTH.

RAINBOW DROPS—SUCK THEM AND YOU CAN SPIT IN SIX DIFFERENT COLORS.

"Come on, come on!" cried Mr. Wonka. "We can't wait all day!"

"Isn't there a *Television Room* in all this lot?" asked Mike Teavee.

"Certainly there's a television room," Mr. Wonka said. "That button over there." He pointed with his finger. Everybody looked. TELEVISION CHOCOLATE, it said on the tiny label beside the button.

"*Whoopee!*" shouted Mike Teavee. "That's for me!" He stuck out his thumb and pressed the button. Instantly, there was a tremendous whizzing noise. The doors clanged shut and the elevator leaped away as though it had been stung by a wasp. But it leapt *sideways*! And all the passengers (except Mr. Wonka, who was holding onto a strap from the ceiling) were flung off their feet onto the floor.

"Get up, get up!" cried Mr. Wonka, roaring with laughter. But just as they were staggering to their feet, the elevator changed directions and swerved violently round a corner. And over they went once more.

"Help!" shouted Mrs. Teavee.

"Take my hand, madam," said Mr. Wonka gallantly.

"There you are! Now grab this strap! Everybody grab a strap. The journey's not over yet!"

Old Grandpa Joe staggered to his feet and caught hold of a strap. Little Charlie, who couldn't possibly reach as high as that, put his arms around Grandpa Joe's legs and hung on tight.

The elevator rushed on at the speed of a rocket. Now it was beginning to climb. It was shooting up and up and up on a steep slanty course as if it were climbing a very steep hill. Then suddenly, as though it had come to the top of the hill and gone over a precipice, it dropped like a stone and Charlie felt his tummy coming right up into his throat, and Grandpa Joe shouted, "Yippee! Here we go!" And Mrs. Teavee cried out, "The rope has broken! We're going to crash!" And Mr. Wonka said, "Calm yourself, my dear lady," and patted her comfortingly on the arm. And then Grandpa Joe looked down at Charlie who was clinging to his legs, and he said, "Are you all right, Charlie?" Charlie shouted, "I love it! It's like being on a roller coaster!" And through the glass walls of the elevator, as it rushed along, they caught sudden glimpses of strange and wonderful things going on in some of the other rooms:

An enormous spout with brown sticky stuff oozing out of it onto the floor. . . .

A great, craggy mountain made entirely of fudge, with Oompa-Loompas (all roped together for safety) hacking huge hunks of fudge out of its sides. . . .

A machine with white powder spraying out of it like a snowstorm. . . .

A lake of hot caramel with steam coming off it. . . .

A village of Oompa-Loompas, with tiny houses and streets and hundreds of Oompa-Loompa children no more than four inches high playing in the streets. . . .

And now the elevator began flattening out again, but it seemed to be going faster than ever, and Charlie could hear the scream of the wind outside as it hurtled forward . . . and it twisted . . . and it turned . . . and it went up . . . and it went down . . . and . . .

"I'm going to be sick!" yelled Mrs. Teavee, turning green in the face.

"Please don't be sick," said Mr. Wonka.

"Try and stop me!" said Mrs. Teavee.

"Then you'd better take this," said Mr. Wonka, and he swept his magnificent black top hat of his head, and held it out, upside down, in front of Mrs. Teavee's mouth.

"Make this awful thing stop!" ordered Mr. Teavee.

"Can't do that," said Mr. Wonka. "It won't stop till we get there. I only hope no one's using the *other* elevator at this moment."

"What other elevator?" screamed Mrs. Teavee.

"The one that goes the opposite way on the same track as this one," said Mr. Wonka.

"Holy mackerel!" cried Mr. Teavee. "You mean we might have a collision?"

"I've always been lucky so far," said Mr. Wonka.

"Now I *am* going to be sick!" yelled Mrs. Teavee.

"No, no!" said Mr. Wonka. "Not now! We're nearly there! Don't spoil my hat!"

The next moment, there was a screaming of brakes, and the elevator began to slow down. Then it stopped altogether.

"Some ride!" said Mr. Teavee, wiping his great sweaty face with a handkerchief.

"Never again!" gasped Mrs. Teavee. And then the doors of the elevator slid open and Mr. Wonka said, "Just a minute now! Listen to me! I want everybody to be very careful in this room. There is dangerous stuff around in here and you *must not* tamper with it."

26
The Television-Chocolate Room

THE TEAVEE FAMILY, together with Charlie and Grandpa Joe, stepped out of the elevator into a room so dazzlingly bright and dazzlingly white that they screwed up their eyes in pain and stopped walking. Mr. Wonka handed each of them a pair of dark glasses and said, "Put these on quick! And don't take them off in here whatever you do! This light could blind you!"

As soon as Charlie had his dark glasses on, he was able to look around him in comfort. He saw a long narrow room. The room was painted white all over. Even the floor was white, and there wasn't a speck of dust anywhere. From the ceiling, huge lamps hung down and bathed the room in a brilliant blue-white light. The room was completely bare except at the far ends. At one of these ends there was an enormous camera on wheels, and a whole army of Oompa-Loompas was clustering around it, oiling its joints and adjusting its knobs and polishing its great glass lens. The Oompa-Loompas were all dressed in the most extraordinary way. They were wearing bright-red space suits, complete with helmets and goggles—at least they looked like space suits—and they were working in complete silence. Watching them, Charlie experienced a queer sense of danger. There was something dangerous about this whole business, and the Oompa-Loompas knew it. There was no chattering or singing among them here, and they moved about over the huge black camera slowly and carefully in their scarlet space suits.

At the other end of the room, about fifty paces away from the camera, a single Oompa-Loompa (also wearing a space suit) was sitting at a black table gazing at the screen of a very large television set.

"Here we go!" cried Mr. Wonka, hopping up and down with excitement. "This is the Testing Room for my very latest and greatest invention—Television Chocolate!"

"But what *is* Television Chocolate?" asked Mike Teavee.

"Good heavens, child, stop interrupting me!" said Mr. Wonka. "It works by television. I don't like television myself. I suppose it's all right in small doses, but children never seem to be able to take it in small doses. They want to sit there all day long staring and staring at the screen. . . ."

"That's me!" said Mike Teavee.

"Shut up!" said Mr. Teavee.

"Thank you," said Mr. Wonka. "I shall now tell you how this amazing television set of mine works. But first of all, do you know how ordinary television works? It is very simple. At one end, where the picture is being taken, you have a large movie camera and you start photographing something. The photographs are then split up into millions of tiny little pieces which are so small that you can't see them, and these little pieces are shot out into the sky by electricity. In the sky, they go whizzing around all over the place until suddenly they hit the antenna on the roof of somebody's house. They then go flashing down the wire that leads right into the back of the television set, and in there they get jiggled and joggled around until at last every single one of those millions of tiny pieces is fitted back into its right place (just like a jigsaw puzzle), and presto!—the photograph appears on the screen. . . ."

"That isn't *exactly* how it works," Mike Teavee said.

"I am a little deaf in my left ear," Mr. Wonka said. "You must forgive me if I don't hear everything you say."

"I said, that isn't *exactly* how it works!" shouted Mike Teavee.

"You're a nice boy," Mr. Wonka said, "but you talk too much. Now then! The very first time I saw ordinary television working, I was struck by a tremendous idea. 'Look here!' I shouted, 'if these people can break up a *photograph* into millions of pieces and send the pieces whizzing through the air and then put them together again at the other end, why can't *I* do the same thing with a bar of chocolate? Why can't *I* send a real bar of chocolate whizzing through the air in tiny pieces and then put the pieces together at the other end, all ready to be eaten?"

"Impossible!" said Mike Teavee.

"You think so?" cried Mr. Wonka. "Well, watch this! I shall now send a bar of my very best chocolate from one end of this room to the other—by television! Get ready, there! Bring in the chocolate!"

Immediately, six Oompa-Loompas marched forward carrying on their shoulders the most enormous bar of chocolate Charlie had ever seen. It was about the size of the mattress he slept on at home.

"It has to be big," Mr. Wonka explained, "because when-ever you send something by television, it always comes out much smaller than it was when it went in. Even with *ordinary* television, when you photograph a big man, he never comes out on your screen any taller than a pencil, does he? Here we go, then! Get ready! *No, no! Stop! Hold everything!* You there! Mike Teavee! Stand back! You're too close to the camera! There are dangerous rays coming out of that thing! They could break you up into million tiny pieces in one second! That's why the Oompa-Loompas are wearing space suits! The suits protect them! All right! That's better! Now, then! *Switch on!*"

One of the Oompa-Loompas caught hold of a large switch and pulled it down.

There was a blinding flash.

"The chocolate's gone!" shouted Grandpa Joe, waving his arms.

He was quite right! The whole enormous bar of choco-late had disappeared completely into thin air!

"It's on its way!" cried Mr. Wonka. "It is now rushing through the air above our heads in a million tiny pieces. Quick! Come over here!" He dashed over to the other end of the room where the large television set was standing, and the others followed him. "Watch the screen!" he cried. "Here it comes! Look!"

The screen flickered and lit up. Then suddenly, a small bar of chocolate appeared in the middle of the screen.

"Take it!" shouted Mr. Wonka, growing more and more excited.

"How can you take it?" asked Mike Teavee, laughing.

"It's just a picture on a television screen!"

"Charlie Bucket!" cried Mr. Wonka. "*You* take it! Reach out and grab it!"

Charlie put out his hand and touched the screen, and suddenly, miraculously, the bar of chocolate came away in his fingers. He was so surprised he nearly dropped it.

"Eat it!" shouted Mr. Wonka. "Go on and eat it! It'll be delicious! It's the same bar! It's gotten smaller on the journey, that's all!"

"It's absolutely fantastic!" gasped Grandpa Joe. "It's . . . it's . . . it's a miracle!"

"Just imagine," cried Mr. Wonka, "when I start using this across the country . . . you'll be sitting at home watching television and suddenly a commercial will flash onto the screen and a voice will say, 'EAT WONKA'S CHOCOLATES! THEY'RE THE BEST IN THE WORLD! IF YOU DON'T BELIEVE US, TRY ONE FOR YOURSELF—*NOW*!' And you simply reach out and take one! How about that, eh?"

"Terrific!" cried Grandpa Joe. "It will change the world!"

27
Mike Teavee Is Sent by Television

MIKE TEAVEE was even more excited than Grandpa Joe at seeing a bar of chocolate being sent by television.

"But Mr. Wonka," he shouted, "can you send *other things* through the air in the same way? Breakfast cereal, for instance?"

"Oh, my sainted aunt!" cried Mr. Wonka. "Don't mention that disgusting stuff in front of me! Do you *know* what breakfast cereal is made of? It's made of all those little curly wooden shavings you find in pencil sharpeners!"

"But could you send it by television if you wanted to, as you do chocolate?" asked Mike Teavee.

"Of course I could!"

"And what about people?" asked Mike Teavee. "Could you send a real live person from one place to another in the same way?"

"A *person*!" cried Mr. Wonka. "Are you off your rocker?"

"But *could* it be done?"

"Good heavens, child, I really don't know . . . I suppose it *could* . . . yes, I'm pretty sure it could . . . of course it could . . . I wouldn't like to risk it, though . . . it might have some very nasty results. . . ."

But Mike Teavee was already off and running. The moment he heard Mr. Wonka saying, "I'm pretty sure it could . . . of course it could," he turned away and started running as fast as he could towards the other end of the room where the great camera was standing. "Look at me!" he shouted as he ran. "I'm going to be the first person in the world to be sent by television!"

"No, no, no, no!" cried Mr. Wonka.

"Mike!" screamed Mrs. Teavee. "Stop! Come back! You'll be turned into a million tiny pieces!"

But there was no stopping Mike Teavee now. The crazy

boy rushed on, and when he reached the enormous camera, he jumped straight for the switch, scattering Oompa-Loompas right and left as he went.

"See you later, alligator!" he shouted, and he pulled down the switch, and as he did so, he leaped out into the full glare of the mighty lens.

There was a blinding flash.

Then there was silence.

Then Mrs. Teavee ran forward . . . but she stopped dead in the middle of the room . . . and she stood there . . . she stood staring at the place where her son had been . . . and her great red mouth opened wide and she screamed, "He's gone! He's gone!"

"Great heavens, he *has* gone!" shouted Mr. Teavee.

Mr. Wonka hurried forward and placed a hand gently on Mrs. Teavee's shoulder. "We shall have to hope for the best," he said. "We must pray that your little boy will come out unharmed at the other end."

"Mike!" screamed Mrs. Teavee, clasping her head in her hands. "Where are you?"

"I'll tell you where he is," said Mr. Teavee, "he's whizzing around above our heads in a million tiny pieces!"

"Don't talk about it!" wailed Mrs. Teavee.

"We must watch the television set," said Mr. Wonka. "He may come through any moment."

Mr. and Mrs. Teavee and Grandpa Joe and little Charlie and Mr. Wonka all gathered round the television and stared tensely at the screen. The screen was quite blank.

"He's taking a heck of a long time to come across," said Mr. Teavee, wiping his brow.

"Oh dear, oh dear," said Mr. Wonka, "I do hope that no part of him gets left behind."

"What on earth do you mean?" asked Mr. Teavee sharply.

"I don't wish to alarm you," said Mr. Wonka, "but it does sometimes happen that only about half the little pieces find their way into the television set. It happened last week. I don't know why, but the result was that only half a bar of chocolate came through."

Mrs. Teavee let out a scream of horror. "You mean only a half of Mike is coming back to us?" she cried.

"Let's hope it's the top half," said Mr. Teavee.

"Hold everything!" said Mr. Wonka. "Watch the screen! Something's happening!"

The screen had suddenly begun to flicker.

Then some wavy lines appeared.

Mr. Wonka adjusted one of the knobs and the wavy lines went away.

And now, very slowly, the screen began to get brighter and brighter.

"Here he comes!" yelled Mr. Wonka. "Yes, that's him all right!"

"Is he all in one piece?" cried Mrs. Teavee.

"I'm not sure," said Mr. Wonka. "It's too early to tell."

Faintly at first, but becoming clearer and clearer every second, the picture of Mike Teavee appeared on the screen. He was standing up and waving at the audience and grinning from ear to ear.

"But he's a midget!" shouted Mr. Teavee.

"Mike," cried Mrs. Teavee, "are you all right? Are there any bits of you missing?"

"Isn't he going to get any bigger?" shouted Mr. Teavee.

"Talk to me, Mike!" cried Mrs. Teavee. "Say something! Tell me you're all right!"

A tiny little voice, no louder than the squeaking of a mouse, came out of the television set. "Hi, Mum!" it said. "Hi, Pop! Look at *me*! I'm the first person ever to be sent by television!"

"Grab him!" ordered Mr. Wonka. "Quick!"

Mrs. Teavee shot out a hand and picked the tiny figure of Mike Teavee out of the screen.

"Hooray!" cried Mr. Wonka. "He's all in one piece! He's completely unharmed!"

"You call *that* unharmed?" snapped Mrs. Teavee, peering at the little speck of a boy who was now running to and fro across the palm of her hand, waving his pistols in the air.

He was certainly not more than an inch tall.

"He's *shrunk*!" said Mr. Teavee.

"Of course he's shrunk," said Mr. Wonka. "What did you expect?"

"This is terrible!" wailed Mrs. Teavee. "What *are* we going to do?"

And Mr. Teavee said, "We can't send him back to school like this! He'll get trod upon! He'll get squashed!"

"He won't be able to do *anything*!" cried Mrs. Teavee.

"Oh, yes I will!" squeaked the tiny voice of Mike Teavee. "I'll still be able to watch television!"

"Never again!" shouted Mr. Teavee. "I'm throwing the television set right out the window the moment we get home. I've had enough of television!"

When he heard this, Mike Teavee flew into a terrible tantrum. He started jumping up and down on the palm of his mother's hand, screaming and yelling and trying to bite her fingers. "I want to watch television!" he squeaked. "I want to watch television! I want to watch television! I want to watch television!"

"Here! Give him to me!" said Mr. Teavee, and he took the tiny boy and shoved him into the breast pocket of his jacket and stuffed a handkerchief on top. Squeals and yells came from inside the pocket, and the pocket shook as the furious little prisoner fought to get out.

"Oh, Mr. Wonka," wailed Mrs. Teavee, "how can we make him grow?"

"Well," said Mr. Wonka, stroking his beard and gazing thoughtfully at the ceiling, "I must say that's a wee bit tricky. But small boys are extremely springy and elastic. They stretch like mad. So what we'll do, we'll put him in a special machine I have for testing the stretchiness of chewing gum! Maybe that will bring him back to what he was."

"Oh, thank you!" said Mrs. Teavee.

"Don't mention it, dear lady."

"How far d'you think he'll stretch?" asked Mr. Teavee.

"Maybe miles," said Mr. Wonka. "Who knows? But he's

going to be awfully thin. Everything gets thinner when you stretch it."

"You mean like chewing gum?" asked Mr. Teavee.

"Exactly."

"How thin will he be?" asked Mrs. Teavee anxiously.

"I haven't the foggiest idea," said Mr. Wonka. "And it doesn't really matter, anyway, because we'll soon fatten him up again. All we'll have to do is give him a triple over-dose of my wonderful Supervitamin Candy. Supervitamin Candy contains huge amounts of vitamin A and vitamin B. It also contains vitamin C, vitamin D, vitamin E, vitamin F, vitamin G, vitamin I, vitamin J, vitamin K, vitamin L, vita-min M, vitamin N, vitamin O, vitamin P, vitamin Q, vitamin R, vitamin T, vitamin U, vitamin V, vitamin W, vitamin X, vit-amin Y, *and*, believe it or not, vitamin Z! The only two vit-amins it doesn't have in it are vitamin S, because it makes you sick, and vitamin H, because it makes you grow horns out of the top of your head, like a bull. But it *does* have in it a very small amount of the rarest and most magical vit-amin of them all—vitamin Wonka."

"And what will *that* do to him?" asked Mr. Teavee anx-iously.

"It'll make his toes grow out until they're as long as his fingers. . . ."

"Oh, no!" cried Mrs. Teavee.

"Don't be silly," said Mr. Wonka. "It's most useful. He'll be able to play the piano with his feet."

"But Mr. Wonka. . . ."

"No arguments, *please*!" said Mr. Wonka. He turned away and clicked his fingers three times in the air. An

Oompa-Loompa appeared immediately and stood beside him. "Follow these orders," said Mr. Wonka, handing the Oompa-Loompa a piece of paper on which he had written full instructions. "And you'll find the boy in his father's pocket. Off you go! Good-by, Mr. Teavee! Good-by, Mrs. Teavee! And please don't look so worried! They all come out in the wash, you know; every one of them. . . ."

At the end of the room, the Oompa-Loompas around the giant camera were already beating their tiny drums and beginning to jog up and down to the rhythm.

"There they go again!" said Mr. Wonka. "I'm afraid you can't stop them singing."

Little Charlie caught Grandpa Joe's hand, and the two of them stood beside Mr. Wonka in the middle of the long bright room, listening to the Oompa-Loompas. And this is what they sang:

> *"The most important thing we've learned,*
> *So far as children are concerned,*
> *Is never, NEVER, NEVER let*
> *Them near your television set—*
> *Or better still, just don't install*
> *The idiotic thing at all.*
> *In almost every house we've been,*
> *We've watched them gaping at the screen.*
> *They loll and slop and lounge about,*
> *And stare until their eyes pop out.*
> *(Last week in someone's place we saw*
> *A dozen eyeballs on the floor.)*

They sit and stare and stare and sit
Until they're hypnotised by it,
Until they're absolutely drunk
With all that shocking ghastly junk.
Oh yes, we know it keeps them still,
They don't climb out the window sill,
They never fight or kick or punch,
They leave you free to cook the lunch
And wash the dishes in the sink—
But did you ever stop to think,
To wonder just exactly what
This does to your beloved tot?
IT ROTS THE SENSES IN THE HEAD!
IT KILLS IMAGINATION DEAD!
IT CLOGS AND CLUTTERS UP THE MIND!
IT MAKES A CHILD SO DULL AND BLIND
HE CAN NO LONGER UNDERSTAND
A FANTASY, A FAIRYLAND!
HIS BRAIN BECOMES AS SOFT AS CHEESE!
HIS POWERS OF THINKING RUST AND FREEZE!
HE CANNOT THINK—HE ONLY SEES!
'All right!' you'll cry. 'All right!' you'll say,
'But if we take the set away,
What shall we do to entertain
Our darling children? Please explain!'
We'll answer this by asking you,
'What used the darling ones to do?
'How used they keep themselves contented
Before this monster was invented?'
Have you forgotten? Don't you know?

We'll say it very loud and slow:
THEY ... USED ... TO ... READ! They'd READ and
    READ,
AND READ and READ, and then proceed
To READ some more. Great Scott! Gadzooks!
One half their lives was reading books!
The nursery shelves held books galore!
Books cluttered up the nursery floor!
And in the bedroom, by the bed,
More books were waiting to be read!
Such wondrous, fine, fantastic tales
Of dragons, gypsies, queens, and whales
And treasure isles, and distant shores
Where smugglers rowed with muffled oars,
And pirates wearing purple pants,
And sailing ships and elephants,
And cannibals crouching 'round the pot,
Stirring away at something hot.
(It smells so good, what can it be!
Good gracious, it's Penelope.)
The younger ones had Beatrix Potter
With Mr. Tod, the dirty rotter,
And Squirrel Nutkin, Pigling Bland,
And Mrs. Tiggy-Winkle and—
Just How The Camel Got His Hump,
And How The Monkey Lost His Rump,
And Mr. Toad, and bless my soul,
There's Mr. Rat and Mr. Mole—
Oh, books, what books they used to know,
Those children living long ago!

So please, oh please, we beg, we pray,
Go throw your TV set away,
And in its place you can install
A lovely bookshelf on the wall.
Then fill the shelves with lots of books,
Ignoring all the dirty looks,
The screams and yells, the bites and kicks,
And children hitting you with sticks—
Fear not, because we promise you
That, in about a week or two
Of having nothing else to do,
They'll now begin to feel the need
Of having something good to read.
And once they start—oh boy, oh boy!
You *watch the slowly growing joy*
That fills their hearts. They'll grow so keen
They'll wonder what they'd ever seen
In that ridiculous machine,
That nauseating, foul, unclean,
Repulsive television screen!
And later, each and every kid
Will love you more for what you did.
P.S. Regarding Mike Teavee,
We very much regret that we
Shall simply have to wait and see
If we can get him back his height.
But if we can't—it serves him right.

28
Only Charlie Left

"WHICH ROOM SHALL IT BE NEXT?" said Mr. Wonka as he turned away and darted into the elevator. "Come on! Hurry up! We *must* get going! And how many children are there left now?"

Little Charlie looked at Grandpa Joe, and Grandpa Joe looked back at little Charlie.

"But Mr. Wonka," Grandpa Joe called after him, "there's . . . there's only Charlie left now."

Mr. Wonka swung round and stared at Charlie.

There was a silence. Charlie stood there holding tightly onto Grandpa Joe's hand.

"You mean you're the *only* one left?" Mr. Wonka said, pretending to be surprised.

"Why yes," whispered Charlie. "Yes."

Mr. Wonka suddenly exploded with excitement. "But my *dear boy*," he cried out, "*that means you've won*!" He rushed out of the elevator and started shaking Charlie's hand so furiously it nearly came off. "Oh, I do congratulate you!" he cried. "I really do! I'm absolutely delighted! It couldn't be better! How wonderful this is! I had a hunch, you know, right from the beginning, that it was going to be you! Well *done,* Charlie, well *done*! This is terrific! Now the fun is really going to start! But we mustn't dilly! We mustn't dally! There's even less time to lose now than there was before! We have an *enormous* number of things to do before the day is out! Just think of the *arrangements* that have to be made! And the people we have to fetch! But luckily for us, we have the great glass elevator to speed things up! Jump in, my dear Charlie, jump in! You too, Grandpa Joe, sir! No, no, *after* you! That's the way! Now then! This time *I* shall choose the button we are going to press!" Mr. Wonka's bright twinkling blue eyes rested for a moment on Charlie's face.

Something crazy is going to happen now, Charlie thought. But he wasn't frightened. He wasn't even nervous. He was just terrifically excited. And so was Grandpa Joe. The old man's face was shining with excitement as he watched every move that Mr. Wonka made. Mr. Wonka was reaching for a button high up on the glass ceiling of the elevator. Charlie and Grandpa Joe both craned their necks to read what it said on the little label beside the button.

It said . . . UP AND OUT.

Up and *out*, thought Charlie. *What sort of a room is that?*

Mr. Wonka pressed the button.

The glass doors closed.

"Hold on!" cried Mr. Wonka.

Then *WHAM*! The elevator shot straight up like a rocket! "Yippee!" shouted Grandpa Joe. Charlie was clinging to Grandpa Joe's legs and Mr. Wonka was holding onto a strap from the ceiling, and up they went, up, up, up, straight up this time, with no twistings or turnings, and Charlie could hear the whistling of the air outside as the elevator went faster and faster. "Yippee!" shouted Grandpa Joe again. "Yippee! Here we go!"

"Faster!" cried Mr. Wonka, banging the wall of the elevator with his hand. "Faster! Faster! If we don't go any faster than this, we shall never get through!"

"Through what?" shouted Grandpa Joe. "What have we got to get through?"

"Aha!" cried Mr. Wonka. "You wait and see! I've been *longing* to press this button for years! But I've never done it until now! I was tempted many times! Oh yes, I was tempted! But I couldn't bear the thought of making a great big hole in the roof of the factory! Here we go, boys! Up and out!"

"But you don't mean . . ." shouted Grandpa Joe, ". . . you don't *really* mean that this elevator. . . ."

"Oh yes, I do!" answered Mr. Wonka. "You wait and see! Up and out!"

"But . . . but . . . but . . . it's made of glass!" shouted Grandpa Joe. "It'll break into a million pieces!"

"I suppose it might," said Mr. Wonka, cheerful as ever, "but it's pretty thick glass, all the same."

The elevator rushed on, going up and up and up, faster and faster and faster. . . .

The suddenly, *CRASH!*—and the most tremendous noise of splintering wood and broken tiles came from directly above their heads, and Grandpa Joe shouted, "Help! It's the end! We're done for!" and Mr. Wonka said, "No, we're not! We're through! We're out!" Sure enough, the elevator had shot right up through the roof of the factory and was now rising into the sky like a rocket, and the sunshine was pouring in through the glass roof. In five seconds they were a thousand feet up in the sky.

"The elevator's gone mad!" shouted Grandpa Joe.

"Have no fear, my dear sir," said Mr. Wonka calmly, and he pressed another button. The elevator stopped. It stopped and hung in mid-air, hovering like a helicopter, hovering over the factory and over the very town itself which lay spread out below them like a picture postcard! Looking down through the glass floor on which he was standing, Charlie could see the small far-away houses and the streets and the snow that lay thickly over everything.

It was an eerie and frightening feeling to be standing on clear glass high up in the sky. It made you feel that you weren't standing on anything at all.

"Are we all right?" cried Grandpa Joe. "How does this thing stay up?"

"Candy power!" said Mr. Wonka. "One million candy power! Oh, look," he cried, pointing down, "there go the other children! They're returning home!"

29
The Other Children Go Home

"WE *MUST* GO DOWN and take a look at our little friends before we do anything else," said Mr. Wonka. He pressed a different button, and the elevator dropped lower, and soon it was hovering just above the entrance gates to the factory.

Looking down now, Charlie could see the children and their parents standing in a little group just inside the gates. "I can only see three," he said. "Who's missing?"

"I expect it's Mike Teavee," Mr. Wonka said. "But he'll be coming along soon. Do you see the trucks?" Mr. Wonka pointed to a line of gigantic covered vans parked in a line nearby.

"Yes," Charlie said. "What are *they* for?"

"Don't you remember what it said on the Golden Tickets? Every child goes home with a lifetime's supply of candy. There's one truckload for each of them, loaded to the brim. Ah-ha," Mr. Wonka went on, "there goes our friend Augustus Gloop! D'you see him? He's getting into the first truck with his mother and father!"

"You mean he's *really* all right?" asked Charlie, astonished. "Even after going up that awful pipe?"

"He's very much all right," said Mr. Wonka.

"He's changed!" said Grandpa Joe, peering down through the glass wall of the elevator. "He used to be fat! Now he's thin as a straw!"

"Of course he's changed," said Mr. Wonka, laughing. "He got squeezed in the pipe. Don't you remember? And look! There goes Miss Violet Beauregarde, the great gum-chewer! It seems as though they managed to de-juice her after all. I'm so glad. And how healthy she looks! Much better than before!"

"But she's purple in the face!" cried Grandpa Joe.

"So she is," said Mr. Wonka. "Ah, well, there's nothing we can do about that."

"Good gracious!" cried Charlie. "Look at poor Veruca Salt and Mr. Salt and Mrs. Salt! They're simply *covered* with garbage!"

"And here comes Mike Teavee!" said Grandpa Joe. "Good heavens! What *have* they done to him? He's about ten feet tall and thin as a wire!"

"They've overstretched him on the gum-stretching machine," said Mr. Wonka. "How very careless."

"But how dreadful for him!" cried Charlie.

"Nonsense," said Mr. Wonka, "he's very lucky. Every basketball team in the country will be trying to get him. But now," he added, "it is time we left these four silly children. I have something very important to talk to you about, my dear Charlie." Mr. Wonka pressed another button, and the elevator swung upwards into the sky.

30
Charlie's Chocolate Factory

THE GREAT GLASS ELEVATOR was now hovering high over the town. Inside the elevator stood Mr. Wonka, Grandpa Joe, and little Charlie.

"How I love my chocolate factory," said Mr. Wonka, gazing down. Then he paused, and he turned around and looked at Charlie with a most serious expression on his face. "Do *you* love it, too, Charlie?" he asked.

"Oh, yes," cried Charlie, "I think it's the most wonderful place in the whole world!"

"I am very pleased to hear you say that," said Mr. Wonka, looking more serious than ever. He went on staring at Charlie. "Yes," he said, "I am very pleased indeed to hear you say that. And now I shall tell you why." Mr. Wonka cocked his head to one side and all at once the tiny twinkling wrinkles of a smile appeared around the corners of his eyes, and he said, "You see, my dear boy, I have decided to make you a present of the whole place.

As soon as you are old enough to run it, the entire factory will become yours."

Charlie stared at Mr. Wonka. Grandpa Joe opened his mouth to speak, but no words came out.

"It's quite true," Mr. Wonka said, smiling broadly now. "I really am giving it to you. That's all right, isn't it?"

"*Giving* it to him?" gasped Grandpa Joe. "You must be joking."

"I'm not joking, sir. I'm deadly serious."

"But . . . but . . . why should you want to give your factory to little Charlie?"

"Listen," Mr. Wonka said, "I'm an old man. I'm much older than you think. I can't go on forever. I've got no children of my own, no family at all. So who is going to run the factory when I get too old to do it myself? *Someone's* got to keep it going—if only for the sake of the Oompa-Loompas. Mind you, there are thousands of clever men who would give anything for the chance to come in and take over from me, but I don't *want* that sort of person. I don't want a grown-up person at all. A grownup won't listen to me; he won't learn. He will try to do things his own way and not mine. So I have to have a child. I want a good sensible loving child, one to whom I can tell all my most precious candy-making secrets— while I am still alive."

"So *that* is why you sent out the Golden Tickets!" cried Charlie.

"Exactly!" said Mr. Wonka. "I decided to invite five children to the factory, and the one I liked best at the end of the day would be the winner!"

"But Mr. Wonka," stammered Grandpa Joe, "do you

really and truly mean that you are giving the whole of this enormous factory to little Charlie? After all. . . ."

"There's no time for arguments!" cried Mr. Wonka. "We must go at once and fetch the rest of the family—Charlie's father and his mother and anyone else that's around! They can all live in the factory from now on! They can all help to run it until Charlie is old enough to do it by himself! Where do you live, Charlie?"

Charlie peered down through the glass elevator at the snow-covered houses that lay below. "It's over there," he said, pointing. "It's that little cottage right on the edge of the town, the tiny little one. . . ."

"I see it!" cried Mr. Wonka, and he pressed some more buttons and the elevator shot down toward Charlie's house.

"I'm afraid my mother won't come with us," Charlie said sadly.

"Why ever not?"

"Because she won't leave Grandma Josephine and Grandma Georgina and Grandpa George."

"But they must come too."

"They can't," Charlie said. "They're very old and they haven't been out of bed for twenty years."

"Then we'll take the bed along as well, with them in it," said Mr. Wonka. "There's plenty of room in this elevator for a bed."

"You couldn't get the bed out of the house," said Grandpa Joe. "It won't go through the door."

"You mustn't despair!" cried Mr. Wonka. "Nothing is impossible! You watch!"

The elevator was now hovering over the roof of the Bucket's little house.

"What are you going to do?" cried Charlie.

"I'm going right on in to fetch them," said Mr. Wonka.

"How?" asked Grandpa Joe.

"Through the roof," said Mr. Wonka, pressing another button.

"No!" shouted Charlie.

"Stop!" shouted Grandpa Joe.

CRASH went the elevator, right down through the roof of the house into the old people's bedroom. Showers of dust and broken tiles and bits of wood and cockroaches and spiders and bricks and cement went raining down on the three old ones who were lying in bed, and each of them thought that the end of the world was come. Grandma Georgina fainted, Grandma Josephine dropped her false teeth, Grandpa George put his head under the blanket, and Mr. and Mrs. Bucket came rushing in from the next room.

"Save us!" cried Grandma Josephine.

"Calm yourself, my darling wife," said Grandpa Joe, stepping out of the elevator. "It's only us."

"Mother!" cried Charlie, rushing into Mrs. Bucket's arms. "Mother! Mother! Listen to what's happened! We're all going back to live in Mr. Wonka's factory and we're going to help him to run it and he's given it *all* to me and . . . and . . . and . . . and. . . ."

"What *are* you talking about?" said Mrs. Bucket.

"Just look at our house!" cried poor Mr. Bucket. "It's in ruins!"

"My dear sir," said Mr. Wonka, jumping forward and shaking Mr. Bucket warmly by the hand, "I'm so very glad to meet you. You mustn't worry about your house. From now on, you're never going to need it again, anyway."

"Who *is* this crazy man?" screamed Grandma Josephine. "He could have killed us all."

"This," said Grandpa Joe, "is Mr. Willy Wonka himself."

It took quite a time for Grandpa Joe and Charlie to

explain to everyone exactly what had been happening to them all day. And even then they all refused to ride back to the factory in the elevator.

"I'd rather die in my bed!" shouted Grandma Josephine.

"So would I!" cried Grandma Georgina.

"I refuse to go!" announced Grandpa George.

So Mr. Wonka and Grandpa Joe and Charlie, taking no notice of their screams, simply pushed the bed into the elevator. They pushed Mr. and Mrs. Bucket in after it. Then they got in themselves. Mr. Wonka pressed a button. The doors closed. Grandma Georgina screamed. And the elevator rose up off the floor and shot through the hole in the roof, out into the open sky.

Charlie climbed onto the bed and tried to calm the three old people who were still petrified with fear. "Please don't be frightened," he said. "It's quite safe. And we're going to the most wonderful place in the world!"

"Charlie's right," said Grandpa Joe.

"Will there be anything to eat when we get there?" asked Grandma Josephine. "I'm starving! The whole family is starving!"

"Anything to *eat*?" cried Charlie, laughing. "Oh, you just wait and see!"

Turn the page
for a look at another
scrumdiddlyumptious
story from

ROALD·DAHL!

Matilda

The Reader of Books

It's a funny thing about mothers and fathers. Even when their own child is the most disgusting little blister you could ever imagine, they still think that he or she is wonderful.

Some parents go further. They become so blinded by adoration they manage to convince themselves their child has qualities of genius.

Well, there is nothing very wrong with all this. It's the way of the world. It is only when the parents begin telling *us* about the brilliance of their own revolting offspring, that we start shouting, "Bring us a basin! We're going to be sick!"

School teachers suffer a good deal from having to listen to this sort of twaddle from proud parents, but they usually get their own back when the time comes to write the end-of-term reports. If I were a teacher I would cook up some real scorchers for the children of doting parents. "Your son Maximilian," I would write, "is a total wash-out. I hope you have a family business you can push him into when he leaves school because he sure as heck won't get a job anywhere else." Or if I were feeling lyrical that day, I might write, "It is a curious truth that grasshoppers have their hearing-organs in the sides of the abdomen. Your daughter Vanessa, judging by what she's learnt this term, has no hearing-organs at all."

I might even delve deeper into natural history and say, "The periodical cicada spends six years as a grub underground, and no more than six *days* as a free creature of sunlight and air. Your son Wilfred has spent six years as a grub in this school and we are still waiting for him to emerge from the chrysalis." A particularly poisonous little girl might sting me into saying, "Fiona has the same glacial beauty as an iceberg, but unlike the iceberg she has absolutely

nothing below the surface." I think I might enjoy writing end-of-term reports for the stinkers in my class. But enough of that. We have to get on.

Occasionally one comes across parents who take the opposite line, who show no interest at all in their children, and these of course are far worse than the doting ones. Mr. and Mrs. Wormwood were two such parents. They had a son called Michael and a daughter called Matilda, and the parents looked upon Matilda in particular as nothing more than a scab. A scab is something you have to put up with until the time comes when you can pick it off and flick it away. Mr. and Mrs. Wormwood looked forward enormously to the time when they could pick their little daughter off and flick her away, preferably into the next county or even further than that.

It is bad enough when parents treat *ordinary* children as though they were scabs and bunions, but it becomes somehow a lot worse when the child in question is *extra*-ordinary, and by that I mean sensitive and brilliant. Matilda was both of these things, but above all she was brilliant. Her mind was so nimble and she was so quick to learn that her ability should have been obvious even to the most half-witted of parents. But Mr. and Mrs. Wormwood were both so gormless and so wrapped up in their own silly little lives that they failed to notice anything unusual about their daughter. To tell the truth, I doubt they would have noticed had she crawled into the house with a broken leg.

Matilda's brother, Michael, was a perfectly normal boy, but the sister, as I said, was something to make your eyes pop. By the age of *one and a half* her speech was perfect and she knew as many words as most grown-ups. The parents, instead of applauding her, called her a noisy chatterbox and told her sharply that small girls should be seen and not heard.

By the time she was *three*, Matilda had taught herself to read by studying newspapers and magazines that lay around the house. At the age of *four*, she could read fast and well and she naturally began hankering after books. The only book in the whole of this enlightened household was something called *Easy Cooking* belonging to her mother, and when she had read this from cover to cover and had learnt all the recipes by heart, she decided she wanted something more interesting.

"Daddy," she said, "do you think you could buy me a book?"

"A *book*?" he said. "What d'you want a flaming book for?"

"To read, Daddy."

"What's wrong with the telly, for heaven's sake? We've got a lovely telly with a twelve-inch screen and now you come asking for a book! You're getting spoiled, my girl!"

Nearly every weekday afternoon Matilda was left alone in the house. Her brother (five years older than her) went to school. Her father went to work and her mother went out playing bingo in a town eight miles away. Mrs. Wormwood was hooked on bingo and played it five afternoons a week. On the afternoon of the day when her father had refused to buy her a book, Matilda set out all by herself to walk to the public library in the village. When she arrived, she introduced herself to the librarian, Mrs. Phelps. She asked if she might sit awhile and read a book. Mrs. Phelps, slightly taken aback at the arrival of such a tiny girl

6

unaccompanied by a parent, nevertheless told her she was very welcome.

"Where are the children's books please?" Matilda asked.

"They're over there on those lower shelves," Mrs. Phelps told her. "Would you like me to help you find a nice one with lots of pictures in it?"

"No, thank you," Matilda said. "I'm sure I can manage."

From then on, every afternoon, as soon as her mother had left for bingo, Matilda would toddle down to the library. The walk took only ten minutes and this allowed her two glorious hours sitting quietly by herself in a cosy corner devouring one book after another. When she had read every single children's book in the place, she started wandering round in search of something else.

Mrs. Phelps, who had been watching her with fascination for the past few weeks, now got up from her desk and went over to her. "Can I help you, Matilda?" she asked.

"I'm wondering what to read next," Matilda said. "I've finished all the children's books."

"You mean you've looked at the pictures?"

"Yes, but I've read the books as well."

Mrs. Phelps looked down at Matilda from her great height and Matilda looked right back up at her.

"I thought some were very poor," Matilda said, "but others were lovely. I liked *The Secret Garden* best of all. It was full of mystery. The mystery of the room behind

the closed door and the mystery of the garden behind the big wall."

Mrs. Phelps was stunned. "Exactly how old are you, Matilda?" she asked.

"Four years and three months," Matilda said.

Mrs. Phelps was more stunned than ever, but she had the sense not to show it. "What sort of a book would you like to read next?" she asked.

Matilda said, "I would like a really good one that grown-ups read. A famous one. I don't know any names."

Mrs. Phelps looked along the shelves, taking her time. She didn't quite know what to bring out. How, she asked herself, does one choose a famous grown-up book for a four-year-old girl? Her first thought was to pick a young teenager's romance of the kind that is written for fifteen-year-old school-girls, but for some reason she found herself instinctively walking past that particular shelf.

"Try this," she said at last. "It's very famous and very good. If it's too long for you, just let me know and I'll find something shorter and a bit easier."

"*Great Expectations*," Matilda read, "by Charles Dickens. I'd love to try it."

I must be mad, Mrs. Phelps told herself, but to Matilda she said, "Of course you may try it."

Over the next few afternoons Mrs. Phelps could hardly take her eyes from the small girl sitting for hour after hour in the big armchair at the far end of the room with the book on her lap. It was necessary to rest it on the lap because it was too heavy for her to hold up, which meant she had to sit leaning forward in order to read. And a strange sight it was, this tiny dark-haired person sitting there with her feet nowhere near touching the floor, totally absorbed in the wonderful adventures of Pip and old Miss Havisham and her cobwebbed house and by the spell of magic that Dickens the great story-teller had woven with his words. The only movement from the reader was the lifting of the hand every now and then to turn over a page, and Mrs. Phelps always felt sad when the time came for her to cross the floor and say, "It's ten to five, Matilda."

During the first week of Matilda's visits Mrs. Phelps had said to her, "Does your mother walk you down here every day and then take you home?"

"My mother goes to Aylesbury every afternoon to play bingo," Matilda had said. "She doesn't know I come here."

"But that's surely not right," Mrs. Phelps said. "I think you'd better ask her."

"I'd rather not," Matilda said. "She doesn't encourage reading books. Nor does my father."

"But what do they expect you to do every afternoon in an empty house?"

"Just mooch around and watch the telly."

"I see."

"She doesn't really care what I do," Matilda said a little sadly.

Mrs. Phelps was concerned about the child's safety

on the walk through the fairly busy village High Street and the crossing of the road, but she decided not to interfere.

Within a week, Matilda had finished *Great Expectations* which in that edition contained four hundred and eleven pages. "I loved it," she said to Mrs. Phelps. "Has Mr. Dickens written any others?"

"A great number," said the astounded Mrs. Phelps. "Shall I choose you another?"

Over the next six months, under Mrs. Phelps's watchful and compassionate eye, Matilda read the following books:

Nicholas Nickleby by Charles Dickens
Oliver Twist by Charles Dickens
Jane Eyre by Charlotte Brontë
Pride and Prejudice by Jane Austen
Tess of the D'Urbervilles by Thomas Hardy
Gone to Earth by Mary Webb
Kim by Rudyard Kipling
The Invisible Man by H. G. Wells
The Old Man and the Sea by Ernest Hemingway
The Sound and the Fury by William Faulkner
The Grapes of Wrath by John Steinbeck
The Good Companions by J. B. Priestley
Brighton Rock by Graham Greene
Animal Farm by George Orwell

It was a formidable list and by now Mrs. Phelps was filled with wonder and excitement, but it was probably a good thing that she did not allow herself to be completely carried away by it all. Almost anyone else witnessing the achievements of this small child would have been tempted to make a great fuss and shout the news all over the village and beyond, but not so Mrs. Phelps. She was someone who minded her own business and had long since discovered it was seldom worth while to interfere with other people's children.

"Mr. Hemingway says a lot of things I don't understand," Matilda said to her. "Especially about men and women. But I loved it all the same. The way he tells it I feel I am right there on the spot watching it all happen."

"A fine writer will always make you feel that," Mrs. Phelps said. "And don't worry about the bits you can't understand. Sit back and allow the words to wash around you, like music."

"I will, I will."

"Did you know," Mrs. Phelps said, "that public libraries like this allow you to borrow books and take them home?"

"I didn't know that," Matilda said. "Could *I* do it?"

"Of course," Mrs. Phelps said. "When you have chosen the book you want, bring it to me so I can make a note of it and it's yours for two weeks. You can take more than one if you wish."

From then on, Matilda would visit the library only once a week in order to take out new books and return the old ones. Her own small bedroom now became her reading-room and there she would sit and read most afternoons, often with a mug of hot chocolate beside her. She was not quite tall enough to reach things around the kitchen, but she kept a small box in the out-house which she brought in and stood on in order to get whatever she wanted. Mostly it was hot chocolate she made, warming the milk in a saucepan on the stove before mixing it. Occasionally she made Bovril or Ovaltine. It was pleasant to take a hot drink up to her room and have it beside her as she sat in her silent room reading in the empty house in the afternoons. The books transported her into new worlds and introduced her to amazing people who lived exciting lives. She went on olden-day sailing ships with Joseph Conrad. She went to Africa with Ernest Hemingway and to India with Rudyard Kipling. She travelled all over the world while sitting in her little room in an English village.

ROALD DAHL

James and the Giant Peach

A little magic can take you a long way!

After James Henry Trotter's parents are tragically eaten by a rhinoceros, he goes to live with his two horrible aunts, Spiker and Sponge. Life there is no fun, until James accidentally drops some magic crystals by the old peach tree and strange things start to happen. The peach at the top of the tree begins to grow, and before long it's as big as a house. Inside, James meets a bunch of oversized friends—Grasshopper, Centipede, Ladybug, and more. With a snip of the stem, the peach starts rolling away, and the great adventure begins!

ROALD DAHL

Charlie and the Great Glass Elevator

Now that he's won the chocolate factory, what's next for Charlie?

Last seen flying through the sky in a giant elevator in *Charlie and the Chocolate Factory*, Charlie Bucket's back for another adventure. When the giant elevator picks up speed, Charlie, Willy Wonka, and the gang are sent hurtling through space and time. Visiting the world's first space hotel, battling the dreaded Vermicious Knids, and saving the world are only a few stops along this remarkable, intergalactic joyride.

ROALD DAHL

Fantastic Mr. Fox

Nobody outfoxes Fantastic Mr. Fox!

Someone's been stealing from the three meanest farmers around, and they know the identity of the thief—it's Fantastic Mr. Fox! Working alone they could never catch him; but now fat Boggis, squat Bunce, and skinny Bean have joined forces, and they have Mr. Fox and his family surrounded. What they don't know is that they're not dealing with just any fox—Mr. Fox would rather die than surrender. Only the most fantastic plan can save him now.

STORIES ARE GOOD FOR YOU.

Roald Dahl said,
"If you have good thoughts, they will shine out of your face like sunbeams and you will always look lovely."

We believe in doing good things.
That's why 10 percent of all Roald Dahl income* goes to our charity partners. We have supported causes including: specialist children's nurses, grants for families in need, and educational outreach programs. Thank you for helping us to sustain this vital work.

Find out more at roalddahl.com